YUSUF FAI

THE CURSE OF TITANIC

THE END OF OCEANGATE
2023

Fadel

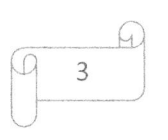

CONTENTS

1. The Titanic: From pride to dream death 12

   Titanic's Construktion and maiden voyage in 1912 12

   The sinking of the Titanic in 1912 15

   J. P. Morgan 20

   Titanic or Olympic? 24

   The discovery of the wreck in 1985 28

   Films and books about the Titanic 31

   A tragedy in the waters of the Baltic Sea 37

   Research and expeditions on the Titanic 42

2. Deadly silence: Submarines at war 44

   The invention of submarines in the First World War 44

   Submarines in the Second World War 47

   Modern submarines for research and wreck searches .. 50

   The last submarine accident off Titan 53

3. Deap-sea Genesis: The Creation of OceanGate 58

   Who came up with the idea for OceanGate? 58

   The founding of the company 62

The development of submarines and diving robots.......64

4. On the trail of the myth: Dives to the Titanic 67

Preparation and equipment 67

Dives to the wreck of the Titanic from 2020..................70

New findings and discoveries 72

Media support and documentation...............................74

5. The curse of the deep: the sinking of the Titan...........77

Presentation of the Titan 2021 submersible..................77

The approval of the Titan for deep dives 85

Previous concerns and incidents.....................................90

Sale of tickets and introduction of the inmates.............96

Start of the expedition to the Titanic.............................99

The bang and the sudden disappearance....................103

The following catastrophe..105

6. Fates of no return: The victims of Titan....................112

Stockton Rush 112

Hamish Harding...116

Shahzada Dawood and Suleman Dawood....................121

Paul-Henry Nargeolet 130

7. Deadly abysses: The search for the truth ... 134

Analysis of the possible causes of the accident ... 134

Technical or human error? ... 138

Conspiracy theories ... 146

The biggest boat accident in migration history ... 155

8. Into the unknown: Marine technology expedition ... 163

Progress with submersibles and robots ... 163

Drones, 3D mapping and virtual tours ... 167

Artificial intelligence and big data from the ocean ... 170

9. Ambition and hope: lessons for eternity ... 172

The future of OceanGate ... 172

The fate of OceanGate after the accident ... 175

Guillermo Söhnlein's Venus Project 2050 ... 177

Exploring the oceans of the future ... 184

The possible disappearance of the Titanic ... 188

Summary of the findings ... 195

Foreword

It is a dark, stormy night in April 1912 and the Titanic, the largest passenger ship of its time and the pride and joy of the White Star Line, is on its maiden voyage from Southampton to New York. There are over 2,200 people on board - first, second and third class passengers as well as the crew. They are all looking forward to the crossing and are full of hope for the future. No one suspects the tragedy that will occur that night.

A tragedy that shocked the world and continues to fascinate to this day. The wreck of the Titanic lies at a depth of over 3800 meters at the bottom of the Atlantic Ocean. For a long time, it was thought to be lost forever. But in 1985 it was rediscovered thanks to modern technology. This opened the door to a new era of exploration. Using submarines and robots, the resting place of the ocean giant can be examined millimeter by millimeter.

One of these submarines bears the name Titan. Built by the company OceanGate, it is specially designed for the exploration of the Titanic. A unique series of expeditions that brings us closer to the wreck than ever before. But also an expedition into history that reminds us of the human tragedy. We look the past in the eye in the hope of learning from it for the future.

The OceanGate team planned over 30 dives in the summer of 2023 to gather new insights into the Titanic. A logistical and technical feat that is only possible with the help of state-of-the-art submarines. The journey to the wreck is a long one - the resting place of the former luxury liner lies around 700 km from the coast of Newfoundland.

At depths of 2000 to 4000 meters, conditions are uncompromising. Diving there requires the utmost precision and extensive safety measures. Even the smallest mistake can have fatal consequences. And yet, ever since the wreck was discovered, it has exerted a magical attraction. Countless researchers and experts have ventured into the deep sea to uncover the secret of the Titanic.

OceanGate is the latest company to demonstrate this daring. With a budget of millions, they are aiming for the seemingly impossible: Regular expeditions to the Titanic to map and document the wreck piece by piece. Never before have they come so close to revealing the full picture of this underwater landscape of ruins.

We are at a turning point in ocean research. With virtual tours and state-of-the-art media technology, we can share these discoveries with the world. Millions of people can experience the Titanic up close without ever setting foot in a submarine. A chance to keep history and memory alive. To honor the dead by telling their story.

Let's climb together through the terrifying ride of the Titan submarine. Let's hold our breath as it glides down into the blue. And let's see what fate will befall the Titan submarine in the depths...

The journey begins!

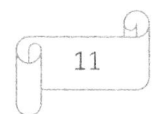

1. The Titanic: From pride to dream death

Titanic's Construktion and maiden voyage in 1912

When the plans for the Titanic were drawn up on the drawing board, they were dreaming a dream - the dream of an unsinkable ship. The Titanic was to be the epitome of luxury, size and safety, a floating palace that could conquer even the roughest seas.

The builders put all their ambition and innovation into this mammoth project. No expense or effort was spared to make this dream a reality. The maiden voyage was looked forward to with pride and confidence. Nothing seemed to be able to stop the steel ocean liner.

But dreams can be shattered. The closer the day of the maiden voyage approached, the more the burden of expectation weighed on the shoulders of the builders. There could be no flaw in this masterpiece of ship engineering. Countless hours of work and ludicrous sums of money went into the construction. Time was running out and the pressure was immense.

Finally, after more than two years, it was done. The Titanic was launched. It was an unparalleled sight as the ship slid into the water! The very last finishing touches were made before the maiden voyage could begin. The excitement reached a climax when the passengers boarded. The who's who of society at the time had gathered to make history on this superlative ship. Now it was time to keep our fingers crossed!

The ship's siren sounded and the ropes were released. Slowly, the colossus began to move, as majestic as a city on the water. The crowd at the harbor waved goodbye. Soon the coast of England was just a strip on the horizon. Set course for New York!

The atmosphere on board was exuberant. People dined and danced as if nothing could dampen the glory of the moment. The Titanic was exactly what they had dreamed of: the ultimate in luxury and technology. Indomitable, she was to cross the ocean and usher in a new era of travel.

But doubts lurked beneath the glittering surface. Would the builders' dream stand up to reality? Or was it doomed to fail, like a house of cards in a storm? It would soon become clear that nothing is truly unsinkable. Not even a dream made of steel...

The sinking of the Titanic in 1912

It is April 14, 1912, shortly before midnight. The Titanic glides through the icy darkness, halfway to New York. The atmosphere on board is exuberant. There is dancing and laughter in the first-class saloon. No one suspects that this luxurious ocean liner will be at the bottom of the Atlantic in just a few hours. Suddenly an alarm sounds through the ship. Lookouts have spotted a huge iceberg directly ahead!

It is too late for an evasive maneuver. The ice scrapes and cuts along the side of the ship with a deafening crash. Icy shivers run down the passengers' limbs. A huge hole now gapes in the starboard hull of the proud ship. Immediately, ice-cold water pours into the lower decks. The watertight bulkheads can only delay the floods, not stop them. The heart of the Titanic, the boiler rooms, threatens to sink. The incomprehensibility of the moment paralyzes the passengers. Only gradually does it become clear: the "unsinkable" ship is going to sink!

A battle against time begins. The few lifeboats are lowered into the water, but there are far too few for everyone. Outside it is freezing cold and panic is growing. Should women and children be rescued first? Or the first-class? Only very few will survive this nightmare.

In the radio room, the operators send desperate distress calls. But the next ships are hours away. They will be too late for most of them. The water is already reaching the upper decks. There is no escape from this maritime inferno.

At around 2:20 a.m. on April 15, the Titanic finally disappears into the black waters. Hundreds have to watch as relatives and friends are swept away to their deaths. Their fate is sealed. The last desperate cries echo across the ocean.

The Carpathia only arrives in the morning and rescues the few survivors. Tears of grief and bewilderment. Everyone has probably lost loved ones. Where there was music and laughter a moment ago, there are now only nameless corpses in life jackets. The biggest maritime disaster in history is complete.

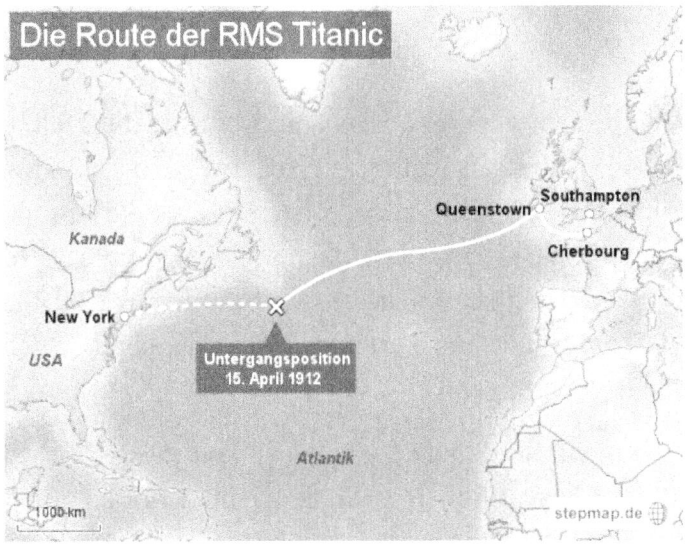

That night, not only did a luxury liner sink, but also the dream of man's technical invincibility. The tragedy claimed more than 1,500 lives - a reminder never to underestimate the forces of nature. And a reminder that, in the end, any pride, no matter how great, is fragile. Even a masterpiece of engineering like the Titanic cannot escape fate.

>>"But there are claims that there was no visible iceberg in the Titanic disaster. How do you see that?" <<

The official version of the sinking is that the Titanic collided near an iceberg, which led to its sinking. This iceberg is said to have been discovered in time by the ship's crew, but it was already too late to prevent a collision. The ship hit the iceberg on the starboard side and suffered severe damage, which led to its sinking.

The theory that there was no visible iceberg is based on various arguments. Some claim that the night was too clear to miss an iceberg and that the crew either made mistakes in identifying the obstruction or deliberately concealed information. It is also claimed that the Titanic may have seen another ship, the RMS Californian, drifting near the iceberg and failed to render assistance.

Another theory is that the Titanic had already been damaged beforehand and that this was concealed in order to preserve the reputation of the ship, which was considered unsinkable. Some even claim that the disaster was planned to cover up insurance fraud or other sinister intentions.

It is important to emphasize that the official version of the sinking of the Titanic is considered credible by many historians and experts. The theory that there was no visible iceberg is often regarded as a conspiracy theory and is based on speculative assumptions and conclusions. Nevertheless, the truth about the visibility of the iceberg in the Titanic disaster remains unclear.

Overall, the story of the Titanic remains one of the most fascinating and tragic stories in maritime history. While there will always be controversy and speculation, the established facts are based on extensive research and comprehensive knowledge about the sinking of this legendary ship. But who was the owner of the Titanic?

J. P. Morgan

John Pierpont Morgan, also known as J. P. Morgan, was an American entrepreneur and the most influential private banker of his time. He was born on April 17, 1837 in Hartford, Connecticut, and died on March 31, 1913 in Rome, Italy. Morgan's father was the banker and financier Junius Spencer Morgan, and his mother was Juliet Pierpont, the daughter of a lawyer and teacher. Morgan studied in Bellerive in the French-speaking canton of Vaud and at the Georg August University in Göttingen from 1856 to 57.

Morgan initially worked in the London branch of his father's company in the banking industry. In 1858, he moved to New York City and later founded the banking house Drexel, Morgan & Company together with Anthony Joseph Drexel, which traded as J. P. Morgan & Company from 1895. Morgan took advantage of the railroad crisis of 1893 to secure financing for the subsequent reorganizations of various railroad companies. He also played a leading role in the creation of the steel trust United States Steel Corp, the world's largest public limited company at the time, through several mergers.

Morgan also invested in the young automotive industry when he contributed two thirds of the share capital of the Maxwell-Briscoe Motor Company. The company became the third largest manufacturer in the USA and later the basis for the Chrysler Corporation. He thus owned the IMMC.

According to his own statements, he attached great importance to the stability and predictability of the conditions.

The Titanic was commissioned by the British shipping company White Star Line and built by the Harland & Wolff shipyard in Belfast. The IMMC also owned the White Star Line, for which the Olympic-class ships, including the Titanic, sailed.

Morgan was originally due to take part in her maiden voyage in April 1912 and was allocated the luxury suite, but he canceled the trip due to scheduling issues. The suite was instead taken by Bruce Ismay, who survived the sinking of the luxury liner.

>>*"Perhaps he knew that the Titanic was going to sink and that's why he didn't go on board. It is claimed that he deliberately let the Titanic sink. His business rivals were also on board. All pure coincidence?"* <<

The theory that J.P. Morgan deliberately caused the sinking of the Titanic is a widespread but highly controversial hypothesis. Objectively speaking, there is no solid evidence to support it:

It is true that Morgan had influence over the White Star Line through his holding company IMMC and was in business competition with some passengers. But that doesn't justify accusing him of something like that.

As a prestige object for the White Star Line, the Titanic was initially lucrative for Morgan, so sabotage seems unlikely. The prominence of many of the victims also speaks against a deliberate intention to kill. In addition, the technology of the time was simply not yet sophisticated enough to carry out such a complex maneuver.

Morgan's absence certainly remains a remarkable coincidence. But ultimately, there is nothing concrete to suggest that he actively influenced the downfall. Even if the idea seems tempting, it is probably a matter of coincidences and rumors that do not stand up to scientific scrutiny.

So without solid evidence, the sabotage theory remains pure speculation. Morgan was certainly unscrupulous in his business dealings, but we should not be too quick to condemn him as a mass murderer.

Titanic or Olympic?

The Olympic, Titanic and Britannic were three British luxury liners built by the White Star Line at the beginning of the 20th century. The Olympic was the first ship and was launched in 1910 and was somewhat damaged. The Titanic followed in 1911, while the Britannic was only completed after the sinking of the Titanic.

Although technically very similar, there were minor structural differences between the three sister ships. The Titanic is considered to be the ship that sank on its maiden voyage in the North Atlantic in 1912.

Nevertheless, the theory persists that the damaged Olympic was secretly sent on its maiden voyage instead of the Titanic so that it could be insured and the company received a large insurance sum. To prove this, details such as porthole arrangements or smokestack markings are cited.

Critics argue that a complete replacement of the ships would have been impossible for logistical and technical reasons.

The controversy cannot be conclusively resolved due to a lack of clear evidence. It remains an exciting, but very questionable theory that has little support among experts.

Despite some inconsistencies, the official theory is that the Titanic sank in 1912, not its sister ship Olympic. Nevertheless, this theory could really be true. But let's leave it at that.

>>"And what happened to the Olympic and the Britannic after the sinking of the Titanic?"<<

After final outfitting work, the Olympic set sail on her maiden voyage from Southampton to New York in June 1911. In the following years, the Olympic served as a passenger and mail ship on the prestigious North Atlantic route.

In September 1911, however, the Olympic collided with the British cruiser Hawke, damaging both ships. After extensive repair work, the Olympic resumed its scheduled service in 1912. In the same year, her sister ship Titanic also sank on her maiden voyage after colliding with an iceberg.

During the First World War, the Olympic served as a troop carrier for a time. In the 1920s and early 1930s, she continued to transport passengers and mail across the Atlantic. However, with increasing age and the Great Depression, operations became unprofitable.

In 1935, the Olympic was decommissioned and then towed to Jarrow in an elaborate maneuver to be scrapped there. From 1936 to 1937, the ship was dismantled and scrapped. Many of the interior fittings were reused or sold.

Her third sister ship, the Britannic, was completed after the sinking of the Titanic. She served in the First World War as a ship specially equipped to provide medical care for the sick and injured, but sank in 1916 after an explosion off the Greek island of Kea. The wreck was not discovered until 1975.

Thus, all three sister ships Olympic, Titanic and Britannic came to an early end - the latter two through their tragic sinkings, the Olympic through being scrapped after more than 20 years of service. They left behind a reputation as milestones of the passenger ship.

The discovery of the wreck in 1985

For over 70 years, the Titanic rested at the bottom of the Atlantic, almost 4,000 meters below the surface of the sea. Its exact location was long considered one of the greatest mysteries of modern times. Numerous expeditions had tried to find the world's most famous shipwreck - so far in vain. But in the summer of 1985, this was to change abruptly.

The American research vessel Knorr set off in search of the legendary ship graveyard using the latest sonar technology. Also on board was the young oceanographer Robert Ballard, driven by his fascination with the Titanic. After all the failed expeditions, would he succeed in discovering the wreck?

On the night of September 1, 1985, the entire crew holds its breath. The screens show strange shadows on the seabed. Is it just a pile of rocks? Or could it actually be the Titanic? Ballard orders a diving drone to be lowered into the water. Hours fly by. Then finally the longed-for images: A huge wreck rises majestically out of the darkness!

Cries of joy break out, tears of emotion flow. The legendary ship has been found! The first pictures show the broken, but still amazingly intact bow. The structure matches the Titanic. The drone glides along the ship's hull and gives an idea of what a colossal wreck lies here in the abyss.

After decades of searching, we have actually succeeded in finding the resting place of this ocean giant! Like a ghost from the depths, the Titanic has returned to the consciousness of mankind. The legendary ship, symbol of an entire era, will never be forgotten. Its history and message will remain etched in our cultural memory.
This sensational discovery marks the beginning of a new era. With the help of modern diving robots, the wreck can now be explored like never before. Piece by piece, the secrets of the Titanic are revealed as she continues to decay at the bottom of the sea.

Robert Ballard's expedition in 1985 made history and fulfilled a long-cherished dream of mankind. The ship's grave in the deep sea is only slowly revealing its treasures and stories. But its fascination is greater than ever today.

Films and books about the Titanic

Hardly any other shipwreck has fascinated people as much as the sinking of the Titanic in 1912, so it's no wonder that filmmakers and authors were inspired by this tragedy so early on.

The first feature film "Atlantic" was released in 1914, two years after the disaster. Further film adaptations followed in the 1930s and 1950s. However, the most elaborate and successful Titanic film to date was "The Last Night of the Titanic" from 1958. The opulent sets conveyed a good picture of the Titanic's appearance.

The breakthrough came in 1997 with James Cameron's "Titanic". With a budget of 200 million dollars, it was the most expensive film of all time. The full-size replica of the luxury liner was sensational.

For the first time, the splendor of the rooms and the tragedy of the sinking could be shown realistically. Cameron also succeeded in creating an emotional connection across the generations through the fictional love story surrounding Jack and Rose. With worldwide box office takings of over 2 billion dollars, "Titanic" became the most successful film in history. The Titanic literature is also extensive. The first reports and eyewitness accounts appeared as early as 1912. In 1955, Walter Lord published the bestseller "A Night to Remember", which was made into a film in 1958. In novels such as "The Last Night of the Titanic" or "Titanic: A Survivor", the story was enriched with fiction.

The real expeditions to the wreck from 1985 onwards provided new impetus, with Robert Ballard and Don Lynch writing "Titanic - The Last Secrets" about their dives. Numerous non-fiction books deal with details of the disaster, biographies of the passengers or the lessons learned from the sinking.

In 2022, the Titanic is still inspiring films such as "Titanic: 25 Years Later". The fascination seems unbroken. Hardly any other event has burned itself so deeply into our culture of remembrance as this sinking of an entire myth. The Titanic lives on - on the big screen, in books and in our minds.

>>"Why is the Titanic still such a big issue after more than 100 years?" <<

When the name Titanic is mentioned today, images immediately spring to mind - the majestic ocean liner, the festively dressed passengers, the tragedy of the icy sinking. Even more than 100 years after the disaster, this luxury liner still exerts an unbroken fascination. But where does the myth of the Titanic come from?

This is certainly partly due to the scale of the disaster. With over 1500 fatalities, the sinking was a tragedy without equal and shocked the world. Never before had man been so brutally reminded of the limits of his supposed omnipotence.

Added to this was the pride and ambition with which the Titanic was celebrated as the most modern ship of its time - unsinkable, invulnerable.

When one of the sailors was asked at the beginning of her maiden voyage whether the ship was really unsinkable, he replied: "God himself could not sink this ship!" The Titanic sank on the same day.

Their demise destroyed this belief in technological progress. It revealed man's vulnerability to the forces of nature. But the fascination goes far beyond the historical tragedy. The stories of the passengers, their hopes and fears still move us today. The struggle for bare survival, the separation from loved ones - it is timelessly human. We can put ourselves in the shoes of those affected.

The romantic component also plays a role. As tragic as the accident was, people are touched by the love between Jack and Rose.
The Titanic remains so topical not least because there are still mysteries. Dives to the wreck have repeatedly brought new details to light. Hightech animations show us the ship more realistically than ever before. It is as if we could still experience the Titanic for ourselves.
This mixture of emotion, myth and mystery has kept the fascination of the Titanic alive for a century. It has become a synonym for the vulnerability of man

and his dreams - and at the same time a reminder never to lose courage and hope.

>>"But in the Wilhelm Gustloff disaster, around 9000 people lost their lives. Why is the Titanic a bigger issue than the ship with the most fatalities? Does the money and the fame of the people play a role? "<<

Yes, it could well be that the social status of the victims played a role in the fact that the sinking of the Titanic is more firmly anchored in the collective memory than the sinking of the Wilhelm Gustloff.

The Titanic was built as a floating luxury hotel for the upper classes of its time. On board were the crème de la crème of society at the time - millionaires, celebrities, industrialists. The sinking and the death of so many rich and famous people naturally attracted a great deal of media attention.

The refugees on the Wilhelm Gustloff, on the other hand, tended to belong to lower social classes. Their fate received less public attention at the time and also later. This selective perception certainly highlights prejudices and distortions in reporting. Objectively speaking, of course, every human life is worth the same, regardless of their social status and the money they possessed.

But your question is justified, that the composition of the victims on the Titanic - the "famous factor" - contributed to the immense preoccupation with this sinking compared to the numerically much larger catastrophe of the Gustloff. But of course that is not correct, the truth is something else.

There is a saying for a reason:
Money rules the world!!!
But what is the Wilhelm Gustloff anyway?

A tragedy in the waters of the Baltic Sea

When the order to evacuate the German civilian population from East Prussia was issued on January 30, 1945 during the Second World War, no one could have imagined the scale of the undertaking. Hundreds of thousands of refugees flocked to the port of Gotenhafen in the hope of escaping the advance of the Red Army by ship.

Among them were women, children and old people, some of whom had only the bare necessities with them. Desperate, they crowded aboard any ship that could take them away from here. One of these ships was the Wilhelm Gustloff, a proud cruise liner that had now been converted into a refugee transport.

However, just hours after departure, in the freezing darkness of the Baltic Sea, death was already lurking. A Soviet submarine fired three torpedoes at the completely overcrowded steamer. Panic broke out as the ship quickly began to list.

People desperately tried to get to safety. But the few lifeboats were nowhere near enough for everyone. Parents were separated from their children as thousands of people were washed out to sea. They barely had a chance of survival in the icy waters. The cries of the drowning people echoed across the sea as the Gustloff sank to the bottom of the Baltic Sea within minutes.

Around 9,000 people died that night, including around 5,000 children, the biggest ship disaster in history.

However, in view of the turmoil of the war, this immeasurable suffering received hardly any public sympathy at the time. It was only later that the fate of the victims was properly commemorated. Today, the Gustloff stands for the senseless tragedy of war, the immeasurable suffering of the civilian population and the value of every human life, regardless of origin. She reminds us that war and hatred should never again produce such horror.

Rescuing the countless victims from the icy Baltic Sea proved to be extremely difficult. Only a few hundred people could be rescued. Many bodies were washed up on the Baltic coast days or weeks later and buried there. The National Socialists exploited the sinking for propaganda purposes and sometimes exaggerated the number of victims. As the ship was also evacuating military personnel, the fate of the children and civilians was pushed into the background for a long time.

The wreck of the Wilhelm Gustloff still lies on the seabed in the Baltic Sea at a depth of around 55 meters. In the decades following the sinking, it was examined several times by divers and underwater cameras in order to reconstruct what happened. The ship's anchor chain was salvaged and unveiled as a memorial.

Literary and cinematic reappraisals only began years after the end of the war. The feature film "Night fell over Gotenhafen" was made in the GDR. Overall, public perception changed: today, the sinking is symbolic of the senseless sacrifices among the civilian population towards the end of the war. However, the question of guilt is considered complex. Commemorative events are now held regularly.

The disaster had little significance in terms of military strategy, but it marked the end of the great passenger ship era. Today, the many fatalities are primarily mourned and seen as an example of the horrors of war.

Research and expeditions on the Titanic

No sooner had the Titanic disappeared into the depths of the Atlantic on April 15, 1912, than speculation about her whereabouts began. Just a few days after the disaster, the Mackay-Bennett set sail to search for survivors and victims. However, this first expedition was unsuccessful. It was not until September 1985 that the research vessel Knorr made the sensational discovery with the help of state-of-the-art sonar equipment. The pictures of the shattered but still astonishingly intact hull went around the world. It was now clear that the Titanic was lying at a depth of 3821 meters, around 650 kilometers off Newfoundland. This was the starting signal for a new era of Titanic research. Expeditions in the 1980s and 90s used high-resolution sonar images and robots to reveal even more details.

In 1994, the Russian research vessel Akademik Keldysh lifted over 1800 artifacts from the seabed.

These included crockery, tiles and other relics, which were published in the magazine article "The Treasure of the Titanic". This controversial salvage operation was the subject of much debate.

In the 2000s, state-of-the-art diving robots and 3D sonar equipment were used. Expeditions such as the one by James Cameron in 2002 or RMS Titanic Inc. provided spectacular images from inside the ship. It was now possible to create walk-through virtual 3D models of the Titanic.

From 2005 onwards, the rate of decay of the wreck increased significantly. In order to safeguard the cultural asset, there were calls for it to be placed under protection. The latest expeditions therefore also serve to document the condition as precisely as possible before the wreck disintegrates completely.

In 2022 and 2023, a particularly large number of missions will take place to mark the 110th anniversary of the sinking. OceanGate worked on a complete mapping and wanted to take tourists to the wreck in submersibles.

2. Deadly silence: Submarines at war

The invention of submarines in the First World War

The first attempts to build boats that could operate underwater date back to the late 19th century. These were based on the inventions of the submersible by the American David Bushnell in 1776 and the first electrically powered submarine by the Spaniard

Isaac Peral in 1886. However, submarine technology was still in its infancy.

The breakthrough came around 1900 with the construction of the first operational German submarine by Rudolf Diesel and Friedrich Krupp. The German navy recognized the potential of this new weapon and had already built 28 submarines by the First World War. They were able to launch torpedoes under their own power for the first time, but were still very slow and had short ranges.

Submarines were used for the first time during the First World War. Germany used them primarily to disrupt supplies from America, which supplied the Allies via the Atlantic. The submarines increasingly operated in organized wolf packs. In 1917, over 1000 Allied ships were sunk.

Development progressed rapidly: larger and more powerful diesel-powered submarines were built that could cruise the oceans. In addition, techniques such as diving and attack procedures were refined. In 1917, the UC-87 was the first submarine to successfully cross the Atlantic.

Overall, submarines revolutionized naval warfare. Their unpredictability and offensive power made them an effective weapon. At the same time, the risky missions at sea claimed many lives. But the foundations of modern submarine warfare had been laid.

After the First World War, submarine construction was severely restricted by the Treaty of Versailles. But their importance had become clear. In the decades that followed, development progressed rapidly right up to nuclear-powered models. Even today, submarines are essential components of navies worldwide.

Submarines in the Second World War

The submarine weapon of the German navy played an important role in the Second World War. After the First World War, submarine construction was severely restricted by regulations, but from 1935 the German navy secretly began building submarines. By 1939, 57 submarines had been built and were ready for use at the start of the war.

Technically, the submarines made great progress compared to the First World War. They now had a design diving depth of over 200 meters and a much greater range thanks to more powerful batteries and diesel engines. The armament with torpedoes and artillery was also greatly improved.

Tactically, the submarines operated in so-called "pack tactics", coordinated groups. This increased the hit rate for convoy attacks. Communication with each other and with the naval command was also simplified by radio.

Particularly during the so-called "happy time" from 1939 to 1941, the U-boats inflicted heavy losses on Allied supply convoys in the North Atlantic and threatened the British Isles. Over 1000 merchant ships were sunk in 1941. The tide only turned with increasing countermeasures such as aircraft support, radar and Enigma decryption.

In total, Germany built over 1100 submarines during the Second World War. They sank over 3000 ships with over 14 million GRT. However, around 780 submarines and around 28,000 crew were also lost. The submarine weapon tied up enormous Allied resources, but did not make a decisive contribution to the outcome of the war.

After the war, German submarine construction was banned again. But their importance for modern warfare had been demonstrated.

Overall, the submarine weapon was a central factor in Germany's war strategy in the Second World War, even if it was not decisive for the war. Their offensive power tied up enormous resources of the enemy. At the same time, its deployment required a high degree of sacrifice on the part of the crews. After the end of the war, the ban on submarines ushered in a new era. However, the underwater battle had revolutionized warfare. Even today, submarines remain feared strategic weapons, even if the framework conditions have changed fundamentally.

Modern submarines for research and wreck searches

After the Second World War, the civilian use of submarines increased rapidly. Instead of military purposes, their suitability for deep-sea scientific expeditions began to be tested. Instead of having torpedoes on board, they were equipped with measuring instruments, gripper arms and diving robots.

In the 1960s, the US Navy built the first non-military deep-sea submarines of the Trieste class. They successfully reached the bottom of the Mariana Trench in 1960 with the Trieste II. Only a little later, the geostationary submarine Alvin also reached milestones such as the exploration of the wreck of the Titanic.

The development of cutting-edge military technology increased enormously during the Cold War. Civilian deep-sea research also benefited from this with a new generation of powerful submersibles. They could now operate autonomously for weeks at a time and dive much deeper than before.

Today, highly specialized submersibles are used in deep-sea research. They are used to map the seabed, take rock samples or investigate wrecks. Modern **sonar technology** enables detailed surveying. Manipulators and robots extend the range of applications.

Companies such as OceanGate develop special submersibles for expeditions to the Titanic or other legendary wrecks. With these high-tech submersibles, private individuals and scientists can now also explore the deep sea. Thanks to improved communication technology, the dives can be broadcast live on the Internet.

Even if many details are still a military secret: Civilian use has turned submarines into high-tech tools for exploring the oceans. The development of new submersibles will enable further groundbreaking expeditions in the future.

>>"What is sonar technology supposed to be?"<<

Sonar technology is a method of locating and examining objects under water. It is based on the principle of sound or ultrasound.

With active sonar, the sonar device itself emits sound or ultrasonic waves that propagate in the water. When the sound hits an object, part of it is reflected back. These echoes are picked up by the sonar and the distance, size, shape and movement of the object can be determined from the transit time or frequency shift (Doppler effect). This is also how the wreck of the Titanic was discovered in 1985.

With passive sonar, the device only listens and analyzes the sound waves coming from other sources such as ships, sea creatures or physical processes. Information can be obtained from the direction and strength of the sound.

In the military, sonar is primarily used to locate enemy submarines. In civilian shipping, it is used to detect obstacles and survey the seabed. In marine research, high-resolution sonar can be used to create sedimentological maps or locate wrecks. Modern sonar systems provide three-dimensional images of the seabed.

The last submarine accident off Titan

When the Indonesian submarine KRI Nanggala left the port of Bali on the morning of April 21, 2021, the mood among the 53-strong crew was relaxed. The almost 60-metre-long German-built submarine was due to take part in a torpedo exercise. Captain Harry Setiawan and his experienced team had carefully prepared the mission. Nobody suspected that the Nanggala was going on its last voyage that day.

At around 3 a.m., the boat reached its destination at a depth of around 700 meters. It submerged for the exercises. But only a few hours later, contact was suddenly lost. When the Nanggala did not report back at the agreed time, the command posts raised the alarm. The search for the 40-year-old submarine immediately began at full speed. What could have happened in the darkness of the deep sea?

Reconnaissance aircraft soon spotted a trail of oil on the surface of the sea - a bad omen for the crew. Marine experts feared the worst. Their fears proved to be true: Four days after the last contact, the Nanggala was broken into three pieces, located on the seabed, at a depth of around 850 meters. There was no hope of rescuing the sailors alive.

In Indonesia, the news of the suspected sinking of the submarine caused shock and grief. Not only the families of the victims through a nightmare. The government also came under political pressure: how could it happen that a dilapidated submarine was sent on a mission? What technical defects led to the disaster? For weeks, experts searched for answers and finally recovered the wreck. The exact circumstances could never be clarified beyond doubt - a power failure, a torpedo false start or simply the boat's decrepitude were all possibilities. The only thing that was certain was that the men had been unable to save themselves. Once again, the sea had taken its toll.

The 53 victims of the KRI Nanggala are a stark reminder. Despite all the progress that has been made, working in the deep remains life-threatening. May their stories never be forgotten. And may their fate teach future generations to face the dangers of the sea with humility.

>>*"But I've never heard of that. How can it be that I see the Titan submarine everywhere in the news and have never heard or seen the Nanggala submarine with over 50 dead?"* <<

There is a reason why you hear more about the Titan

submarine than the Nanggala submarine. The Titan submarine was an American submarine operated by an American company. The Nanggala submarine was an Indonesian submarine operated by the Indonesian Navy.

The USA has a much greater media presence than Indonesia. This means that news from the USA appears more frequently in the news in other countries. In addition, the US is a much richer and more powerful nation than Indonesia. This means that news about the US also appears more prominently in the news in other countries.

The fact that the five occupants of the Titan submarine were rich probably also contributed to the fact that the news about the submarine appeared more frequently. Rich people are often more interesting in the news than poor people. This is because rich people often have power and influence. They are also often better known than poor people.

The fact that the more than 50 occupants of the Nanggala submarine were poor probably contributed to the fact that the news about the submarine appeared less frequently. Poor people are often less interesting in the news than rich people. This is because poor people often lack power and influence. They are also often less well known than rich people.

That's just a fact and of course it's inhuman. But is it still the case? For the most part, yes! And can we do anything about it? I don't think so

We should just know that the media could often convey what they think is important news or even give false information to the public to take advantage of it. Remember:
Money rules the world!!!

3. Deap-sea Genesis: The Creation of OceanGate

Who came up with the idea for OceanGate?

Stockton Rush and Guillermo Söhnlein came up with the idea for OceanGate. Rush is an experienced submarine pilot and oceanographer, while Söhnlein is an entrepreneur and investor. The two founders share the vision of making the deep sea accessible to a wider audience.

Rush has always had a dream of exploring the deep sea. He was born in Seattle, Washington, and spent his childhood diving and snorkeling in the waters of Puget Sound. He soon amassed a collection of shells, snails and other sea creatures.

After graduating from high school, Rush studied at the University of Washington and graduated with a Bachelor of Science in Aeronautical Engineering. He then worked as a submarine pilot for a number of companies, including the Woods Hole Oceanographic Institution and the National Oceanic and Atmospheric Administration. He has dived in the depths of the Pacific Ocean, Indian Ocean and Atlantic Ocean, investigating sea floors, hydrothermal vents and underwater mountains.

In 2009, Rush decided to realize his dream and founded OceanGate with Guillermo Söhnlein. Söhnlein is an entrepreneur and investor interested in deep sea exploration. He is also a former naval officer and has experience in developing and managing companies.

Rush and Söhnlein share a vision of making the deep sea accessible to a wider audience. They believe that the deep sea is a treasure trove of wonders that should be explored by all. They founded OceanGate to make this vision a reality.

The company offers expeditions that give people the opportunity to experience the deep sea first-hand. The expeditions are led by a team of experienced scientists and submarine pilots and are designed to give participants the opportunity to explore the deep sea and experience the wonders that lie hidden there.

OceanGate has already conducted many expeditions and gained many new insights into the deep sea. OceanGate's expeditions have also helped to raise awareness of the importance of the deep sea and have led to greater exploration of the deep sea.

Stockton Rush and Guillermo Söhnlein are visionary entrepreneurs who are helping to better understand and protect the deep sea. Their work will help to make the deep sea accessible to a wider audience and raise awareness of the importance of the deep sea.

The founding of the company

The founding of OceanGate was the result of a shared vision of two entrepreneurs who loved and wanted to explore the oceans. Stockton Rush and Guillermo Söhnlein were both fascinated by the deep sea and its mysteries. They also had an entrepreneurial streak and wanted to create something new and meaningful.
Stockton Rush was an engineer and pilot who dreamed of space travel and ocean exploration as a child. He studied aerospace engineering at Princeton University and later worked for various companies in the aerospace industry. He was also an avid diver and sailor who traveled to many places around the world.

Guillermo Söhnlein was a lawyer and investor interested in the development of new technologies and markets. He studied law at Georgetown University and later worked for various companies in the internet, biotechnology and energy sectors. He was also a passionate adventurer who climbed Mount Everest, among other things.

The two met at a conference on commercial space travel in 2008. They realized that they had a lot in common, especially their love of the ocean and their desire to explore it. They decided to work together and found a company that offered deep-sea submersibles that were accessible to everyone.

They named their company OceanGate and founded it in Everett, Washington, in 2009. Their goal was to democratize access to the deep sea for scientists, journalists, filmmakers and adventurers by offering affordable and safe submersibles. They believed that the deep sea offered untapped potential for discovery, education and inspiration.

They initially financed their company from their own funds and then looked for investors and partners who shared their vision. They also recruited a team of engineers, designers, divers and operators to work on the development and operation of their submersibles.

The development of submarines and diving robots

Their first submersible was the Cyclops 1, a steel submersible for five people that could dive to depths of up to 500 meters. They used it for various projects, such as exploring coral reefs, shipwrecks and underwater volcanoes. They also worked with various partners, such as the University of Washington, the Monterey Bay Aquarium Research Institute and the National Oceanic and Atmospheric Administration.

Their second submersible was the Titan, originally called Cyclops 2, a deep-sea submersible for five people that could dive to depths of up to 4,000 meters. It was the first submersible of its kind to be made of carbon fiber and titanium instead of steel or aluminum. These materials were lighter, stronger and more resistant to corrosion than conventional metals. They allowed the submersible to withstand the enormous pressure of the deep sea without adding too much weight or bulk.

The Titan was completed in 2018 and completed several test voyages in various waters. Among other things, it was used for diving trips to the wreck of the Titanic passenger liner, which sank in 1912 and lies at a depth of around 3,800 meters. The Titanic was one of the most famous and fascinating wrecks in world history and attracted many visitors who wanted to learn more about its history.

The Titan was the only commercial submersible to offer such expeditions. It had a large acrylic glass dome that gave the occupants a 180-degree view of the underwater world. It was also equipped with a sonar system, a high-speed data link and an artificial intelligence called Watson, which acted as a virtual assistant.

The Titan was considered a groundbreaking innovation in deep-sea research and received much praise and recognition from experts and the media. It was described as "the most advanced manned research submarine in the world" and celebrated as "a new era in ocean exploration".

4. On the trail of the myth: Dives to the Titanic

Preparation and equipment

We are in 2012 and the preparations for OceanGate's expedition to the Titanic were lengthy and complex. The company had to put together a team of experienced scientists and submarine pilots, procure suitable equipment and draw up a detailed safety protocol.

The OceanGate team consisted of 12 people, including two submarine pilots who controlled the submarine remotely, two scientists and eight other crew members. The scientists were experts in oceanography, geology and archaeology. They were entrusted with the task of examining the wreck of the Titanic and documenting the findings. The crew members were responsible for the maintenance of the submarine and the safety of the team.

OceanGate's equipment consisted of two diving robots and a large number of sensors. It can dive to depths of up to 10,000 meters. The submarine is equipped with a range of cameras, sonar and other sensors that enable scientists to investigate and document the wreck of the Titanic. The diving robots are smaller than DeepSea and can enter narrow areas that are too dangerous for the submarine. The sensors are used to monitor the submarine's surroundings.

OceanGate's expedition to the Titanic was a complete success. The diving robot was able to explore the wreck of the Titanic and gain a wealth of knowledge. The team's findings have been published in a number of scientific publications and have helped to improve our understanding of the Titanic and the deep sea.

The OceanGate expedition was a milestone in the history of deep-sea research. It was the first expedition to investigate the wreck of the Titanic with a submarine. The team's findings have helped to improve our understanding of the Titanic and the deep sea.

Dives to the wreck of the Titanic from 2020

In 2020, the time had come: the specially built submersibles Titan and Cyclops 2 set off on the first manned expedition to the wreck of the Titanic since 2005. A Herculean task: the wreck lies at a depth of 3780 meters off the coast of Newfoundland - a deadly environment that places the highest demands on technology and crew.

The OceanGate submersibles are equipped with the latest technology to meet these requirements: Radar and high-resolution cameras, grab arms for sampling, laser scanning. Each expedition was meticulously planned and manned by an expert team of divers, engineers and researchers.

In 2020, high-resolution 4K and 3D images of the wreck were taken for the first time, revealing breathtaking details. Over the following years, laser scans and photogrammetry were used to create 3D models accurate to the millimeter. Robotic arms helped to remove corroded samples from the outer hull and analyze the decay processes.

The aim was to document the wreck of the Titanic as accurately as possible before its inevitable decay. At the same time, these dives also made it possible to travel back in time. Historical relics such as crockery and tile fragments provided insights into the sinking and life on board. Virtual tours brought the wreck to life for millions of people.

The OceanGate expeditions between 2020 and 2023 wrote a new chapter in the exploration of the Titanic. Never before had the wreck been mapped and examined in such detail. These unique missions saved the Titanic myth from oblivion - and at the same time awakened a fascination for the unknown depths of the oceans.

New findings and discoveries

When OceanGate launched its first manned expedition to the wreck of the Titanic in over 15 years in 2020, the expectations were enormous. Could state-of-the-art technology really be used to gain new insights into this historic treasure at the bottom of the sea? The results were to exceed all expectations.

The very first dives in 2020 delivered high-resolution 4K and 3D images, revealing breathtaking details that had previously been hidden in the shadows. The camera shots along the outer hull and the bow section in particular showed the extent of the wreck's weathering and resolution. But the astonishing intactness of some areas also became visible.

In the years that followed, the latest photogrammetry and laser scans were used to create 3D models accurate to the millimetre, documenting the size and nature of the wreck in greater detail than ever before. Important structural features such as the arrangement of the portholes or the funnels were precisely measured and mapped.

The examination of material science samples from the outer hull and equipment was particularly revealing. The analysis of corrosion and metal oxidation provided an insight into the complex chemical and biological decay processes of the wreck in the deep sea. DNA analyses of microbes were also carried out.

As research progressed, more and more detailed reconstructions of the sinking chronology were made. It was also possible to locate many personal and historical finds, which allowed conclusions to be drawn about life on board. The fate of the passengers and crew became more tangible.

The OceanGate expeditions have enriched our knowledge of the Titanic enormously in just a few years. New technologies have opened up completely new perspectives on the myth and made it more tangible than ever. The discoveries will shape our image of the Titanic for a long time to come. And there is no doubt that the wreck still holds countless secrets for future expeditions.

Media support and documentation

One of the pioneering features of the OceanGate expeditions to the Titanic was the intensive digital documentation and real-time media coverage. This made it possible to share this modern exploration of the famous shipwreck with an audience of millions worldwide.

Even the early missions from 2020 onwards were recorded by camera teams in image and sound. The breathtaking footage of the wreck in 4K resolution was transmitted directly to the surface and made available on the internet via live streams. This allowed the whole world to follow the dives on the Titanic at the same time.

In the years that followed, the technical transmission and 3D reconstruction were continuously improved. In 2021, virtual reality goggles were even used for a dive, allowing even more intensive immersion. The phantom cameras delivered impressive 12K images. Artificial intelligence helped to process the huge amounts of data and transform them into vivid 3D models.

Public relations work was also greatly expanded. In TV documentaries, videos and podcasts, OceanGate provided insights into the meticulous planning and preparation of the expeditions. The media and social interest was overwhelming. Thousands of applications were received for the coveted places on board the diving boats.

Social media channels, a constantly updated website and press and blog articles rounded off the comprehensive documentation. The expeditions thus became part of our digital lives - and brought the fascination for the deep sea into the living rooms of the world. This superior media support will go down in the history books as a milestone.

PS: You are also welcome to watch videos about virtual tours inside the Titanic to get a clear picture of the Titanic's interior.

5. The curse of the deep: the sinking of the Titan

Presentation of the Titan 2021 submersible

Let's get to the exciting part. The Titan submarine was originally called Cyclops 2 and was a submarine from OceanGate. It was made of carbon fiber and titanium to create a lightweight and robust submarine. It was completed in 2021 and used for diving trips to the wreck of the Titanic. It had a length of 6.7 meters, a width of 3 meters, a height of 2.3 meters and weighed just under 10 tons.

It could accommodate up to 5 people sitting in a titanium pressure chamber. The pressure chamber had a diameter of 2.1 meters and was equipped with an acrylic glass viewing window. The Titan was powered by an electric motor that turned four propellers. It could dive to depths of up to 4,000 meters and had a speed of up to 6 km/h. To navigate to its destination, the Titan was dependent on support from the escort ship, which monitored the Titan's course and communicated course corrections. For this purpose, the boat was equipped with a transponder that enabled the escort ship to locate it. As radio waves are too strongly attenuated under water and are therefore unsuitable, communication and coordination between the escort ship and Titan took place via acoustic underwater telephony - in other words, short text messages were converted into acoustic signals and translated back after transmission. The Titan was an innovative and unique submersible, but it came with some risks.

The use of carbon fiber made the submarine lighter, but also more susceptible to damage from salt water or collisions. The pressure chamber could only be opened from the outside, which made it difficult to rescue passengers in an emergency. In addition, the Titan was not designed for long-term use, but rather as an experimental submarine. Stockton Rush, was the main man responsible for the design and construction of the Titan. He admitted that he "broke some rules" by making the submarine out of carbon fiber and titanium instead of metal like most other submarines.

>>"And why do you do that when he know it's wrong?"<<

There are various reasons why people break rules, depending on the situation and the person. Some people break rules because they believe they will get an advantage or a reward, or because they think the rules are unfair or pointless. Other people break rules because they want to adapt to the circumstances or be creative. Still others break rules because they act impulsively or are guided by their emotions.

In the case of Stockton Rush, the CEO of OceanGate, he said that he broke the rules because he wanted to build an innovative and powerful submarine that could explore the Titanic. He believed that carbon fiber and titanium were better materials than metal to withstand the high pressure at depth. But the submarine experts disagree.

>>"And is it true that he really only steered his submarine with a cheap controller?"<<

Yes, if you can put it that way. The Titan submarine was controlled with a Logitech F710 Wireless gamepad, which was connected to the submarine via Bluetooth. The crew in the submarine received text messages from a mother boat and then used the controller to steer the submarine. Stockton Rush explained that he chose the controller, because it was easy to use and reliable.

>>"How can he think like that. The controller often disconnects when I play with it and he uses it for a submarine. I bought the thing for 40$. What is he thinking?"<<

I understand that you think the controller is a bad choice. But Stockton Rush had his reasons. He said he chose the controller because it was easy to use and reliable. He also said that he had used the controller for years on other subs and had never had any problems with it. He said that the controller was better than a complicated control panel with lots of buttons and levers. Personally, I'm right there with you, you should at least have an emergency control installed in the submarine, even if he thinks it's better with the Xbox controller. But maybe the controller wasn't the problem, who knows.

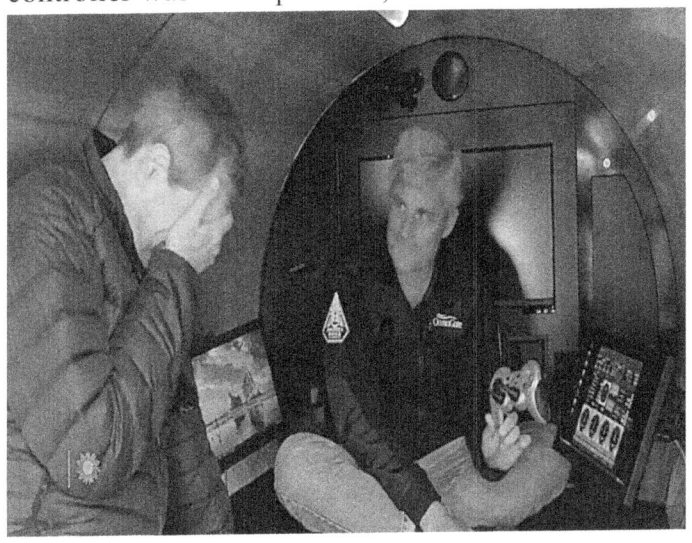

When he presented his 2022 submarine on YouTube, he received quite a lot of criticism, especially on the internet. Many people made fun of him or asked how he could steer such an important project with a cheap toy.

However, the development and production of such highly specialized deep-sea submersibles is certainly associated with very high costs.

Based on a few indications, it can be roughly estimated that the production costs of the Titan submersible were in all probability in the high single-digit millions:

- The development and construction took around 2-3 years.
- Highly qualified engineering and production personnel were involved.
- Extensive systems such as air supply, electricity, navigation etc. had to be developed.
- The materials used, such as carbon fiber and special glass, are very cost-intensive.
- Extensive tests and optimizations were necessary
- As a one-off prototype, titanium was probably more expensive than later models.

Overall, it is therefore very plausible that the production costs amounted to a few million USD.

But rightly so, if you want to dive that deep, you should definitely put a lot on the table. He shouldn't have skimped on an emergency control system.

The approval of the Titan for deep dives

As the Titan operated in international waters and did not carry passengers from a port, it was not subject to any safety regulations. The ship was not certified as seaworthy by any regulatory agency or third-party organization. Reporter David Pogue, who completed the expedition in 2022 as part of a CBS News Sunday Morning feature, said that all passengers boarding Titan sign a waiver acknowledging that it is an "experimental" vessel "that has not been approved or certified by any regulatory agency and could result in bodily injury, disability, mental trauma or death." Television producer Mike Reiss, who also conducted the expedition, said the waiver "mentions death three times on page one." In a 2019 article published in Smithsonian Magazine, Rush was described as a "swashbuckling inventor". The article describes Rush as having said that the U.S. Passenger Vessel Safety Act of 1993 "unnecessarily prioritizes passenger safety over commercial innovation". In an interview from 2022, Rush told CBS News, "At some point, safety is just a waste." I mean, if you just want to be safe, don't get out of bed. Don't get in your car. Don't do anything." Rush said in a 2021 interview, "I broke some rules to make (Titan). I think I broke them with logic and good engineering behind it. Carbon fiber and titanium, there's one rule you don't do. Well, I did."

OceanGate claimed that Titan was the only manned submersible to use RTM, an integrated real-time health monitoring system. The proprietary system, patented by Rush, used acoustic sensors and strain gauges at the pressure boundary to analyze the effects of rising pressure as the watercraft ventured deeper into the ocean and to monitor the integrity of the hull in real time. This is to provide early warning of problems and allow sufficient time to abort the descent and return to the surface.

The Titan's first dive was a complete success. The crew was able to explore a huge deep-sea reef that had never been seen by humans before. The reef was full of life, with colorful fish, corals and other sea creatures. The crew was impressed by the beauty and diversity of the reef. The dive was an important milestone for OceanGate. It showed that the Titan is a powerful tool for deep-sea exploration.

OceanGate's expeditions will help to improve our understanding of the deep sea and protect its biodiversity.

>>"*What? How is it that he didn't have to get any approvals or safety regulations for his submarine when everyone knew he had broken the rules in terms of the materials used and even used an Xbox "***** controller" as a controller?*"<<

Always take it easy.
 There are some reports suggesting that the Titan did not undergo adequate safety tests prior to the dive to the Titanic and that several experts and former OceanGate employees have warned of potential problems with the submarine.

According to a former OceanGate employee, who wished to remain anonymous, the Titan had only passed a single pressure test, but not a test at a depth of 3800 meters, where the wreck of the Titanic lies.

He also said that the Titan had several technical defects, such as a leaking hatch, a faulty battery and a faulty communication system.

Also, in 2018, a letter was sent to OceanGate's CEO, Stockton Rush, from industry leaders in the subsea vehicle field warning him of possible "catastrophic" consequences if he deployed the Titan without proper testing and certification. They said that the Titan did not meet International Marine Contractors Association (IMCA) standards and that they feared he would "kill someone".

Finally, the New York Times reported that several experts in the field of deep-sea exploration had expressed concerns about the Titan's safety and that some of them had even canceled their participation in the expedition. They said that the Titan was built too quickly, had been tested too little and posed too many risks.

So it seems that there were some indications that the Titan had not passed a safety test and that some people had said something. But for some reason

OceanGate ignored those warnings or didn't take them seriously. That is very unfortunate and tragic.

It remains to be seen and hoped that OceanGate's submarines will be approved for commercial use in the future. If they are approved, they will probably be subject to the strictest safety standards.

Previous concerns and incidents

In 2018, David Lochridge, Director of Marine Operations at OceanGate, wrote a report documenting the safety concerns he had about titanium. In court documents, Lochridge said he had urged the company to have titanium assessed and certified by an agency, but OceanGate had refused on the grounds that he was unwilling to pay. He also said that due to its non-standard and therefore experimental design, the transparent viewing window at its forward end was only certified to a depth of 1,300m, only a third of the depth required to reach the Titanic. According to Lochridge, RTM would only indicate when a component was about to fail - often milliseconds before an implosion and could not detect existing flaws in the hull until it was too late. Lochridge was also concerned that OceanGate would not perform non-destructive testing on the hull before undertaking crewed dives, claiming that he was repeatedly told that no scan of the hull or bond line could be performed to check for delamination, porosity and voids of sufficient adhesion of the adhesive used due to the thickness of the hull.

OceanGate advised that Lochridge, who was not an engineer, had refused to accept safety approvals from OceanGate's engineering team and that the company's evaluation of the Titan hull was stronger than any third-party evaluation Lochridge believed was necessary. OceanGate sued Lochridge for alleged breach of its confidentiality contract and fraudulent statements. Lochridge countersued, claiming that he was wrongfully terminated for raising concerns about Titan's ability to operate safely. The two parties settled a few months later.

Later in 2018, the Marine Technology Society wrote a letter to Stockton Rush expressing unanimous concern about the development of TITAN and the planned Titanic expedition, pointing out that the current experimental approach, "could lead to negative outcomes (ranging from minor to catastrophic) that would have serious consequences for everyone in the industry. One signer of the letter later told the New York Times that Rush called him after reading it to tell him that he believed industry standards were stifling innovation.

In March 2018, Rob McCallum, a leading deep-sea exploration specialist, emailed Rush to warn him that he was potentially risking the safety of his clients and advised against using the submersible for commercial purposes until it had been independently tested and classified: "I implore you to exercise all due diligence and be very, very conservative in your testing and sea trials." Rush replied that he was fed up with industry players trying to use a safety argument to stop innovation. We've heard the gratuitous cries of 'you're going to kill someone' far too often. I take that as a grave personal insult. McCallum then sent Rush another email saying, "I think you may be putting yourself and your customers in a dangerous dynamic. In your race to the Titanic, you echo the famous cry, "**She is unsinkable**". This prompted the lawyers at OceanGate to threaten McCallum with legal action.

In 2022, British actor and TV presenter Ross Kemp, who had previously taken part in deep-sea dives for TV channel Sky History, had planned to mark the 110th anniversary of the sinking of the Titanic with a documentary in which he would take Titan on a dive to the wreck. Kemp's agent Jonathan Shalit said the project was put on hold after production company Atlantic Productions deemed the submersible unsafe and not fit for purpose.

Previous incidents

In 2022, reporter David Pogue was aboard the surface ship when the Titan was lost and was unable to locate the **Titanic** during a dive. Pogue's December 2022 report for CBS News Sunday Morning, which questioned the Titan's safety, went viral on social media after the submersible lost contact with its support ship in June 2023. In the report, Pogue commented to Rush that it appears this submersible has some elements of MacGyvery-jerry-rigged-ness. "MacGyvery-jerry-rigged-ness" is a term that refers to the ability to find a solution to a problem by working creatively and improvising with whatever materials are at hand. The term "MacGyvery" comes from an American television series from the 1980s in which the protagonist, Angus MacGyver, was known for his ability to solve complex problems with simple objects. "Jerry-rigged" is a colloquial expression that refers to a makeshift or makeshift repair done with improvised means. He said a $40 Logitech F710 wireless game controller with modified joysticks was used to steer and pitch the submersible, and construction tubes were used as ballast.

On another dive to Titanic in 2022, one of Titan's thrusters was accidentally installed backwards and the submersible began spinning in circles as it tried to move forward near the seabed. As documented in the BBC documentary "Take Me to Titanic", the problem was circumvented by steering while holding the game controller sideways. According to court documents from November 2022, OceanGate reported that the submersible suffered from battery problems during a dive in 2022 and as a result had to be manually attached to a lifting platform, resulting in damage to external components.

Sale of tickets and introduction of the inmates

The trip was booked in early 2023. Rush approached Las Vegas businessman Jay Bloom with two discounted tickets, intending to accompany him and his son on the trip. The billionaire was offered a price of $150,000 per seat instead of the full price of $250,000, with Rush claiming it was "safer than crossing the street", but Bloom declined the offer due to safety concerns. At the time, the trip was scheduled for May, but bad weather delayed it until June.

On its website, the company OceanGate offered the opportunity to take part in an expedition to the Titanic. Interested parties had to apply online and complete a questionnaire in which they stated their motivation, experience and expectations. The company then selected the participants they felt were best suited, both as explorers and adventurers. The selection criteria were not publicly known, but it was thought that the company was primarily looking for people who had a passion for the Titanic and were willing to take a risk.

The tickets were sold from 2019 and initially cost 125,000 US dollars. In 2023, the company increased the price to 250,000 US dollars, presumably due to high demand and rising costs. The company claimed that the expeditions were not commercial, but had a scientific purpose.

The expeditions were to take place in June 2023 and last four days each. The participants were taken by ship from Newfoundland to the wreck site and then transferred to the Titan submarine. The submarine could take up to five people: the captain, the pilot, a researcher and two paying passengers. The journey to the wreck was to take around three hours and the passengers would have seen the Titanic up close.

The Titan's occupants were a colorful mix of different countries, professions and backgrounds. However, they all shared a fascination for the Titanic and a desire for an extraordinary experience. Among them, for example, was a British entrepreneur, pilot and adventurer who lived in the United Arab Emirates. He was the founder of the Action Group, an international aircraft broker. He was also a world record holder for various flying and diving feats. A French deep-sea explorer and Titanic expert was also on board, a businessman and investor from Pakistan along with his 19-year-old son and the CEO of OceanGate, Stockton Rush himself. They had all paid a lot of money to realize their dream.

Start of the expedition to the Titanic

The OceanGate Titanic Expedition was a series of 18 dives that were to take place in the summer of 2023 to explore and document the wreck of the Titanic. The expedition cost 250,000 US dollars per person. The crew of the Titan consisted of five people: Stockton Rush, the founder and CEO of OceanGate. British entrepreneur and pilot Hamish Harding. The French marine researcher and Titanic expert Paul Henry Nargeolet Aka. (Mr. Titanic) and the Pakistani managing director and investor

Shahzada Dawood together with his 19-year-old son Suleman Dawood.

On June 16, 2023, the expedition to the Titanic started aboard the research and expedition ship MV Polar Prince in St. John's, Newfoundland. The ship arrived at the dive site on June 17. One of the occupants, Hamish Harding, posted on Facebook: < Due to the worst winter in Newfoundland in 40 years, this mission will likely be the first and only manned mission to the Titanic in 2023. A weather window has just opened and we will attempt a dive tomorrow >. He also pointed out that the operation was scheduled to begin the next day, June 18, around 4:00 a.m. in America (EDT), which is 08:00 a.m. in Europe (UTC). The dive operation began on June 18 at 9:30 a.m. Newfoundland Daylight Saving Time (NDT) or 12:00 p.m. in Europe (UTC).

With a final metallic groan, the Titan's hatch closed. Stockton Rush looked around at his crew - history was about to be made today. "Prepare to descend!" His voice rumbled through the cramped interior. With a jerk, the submarine began to move, down into the black darkness of the Atlantic Ocean. Centimetre by centimetre, the Titan advanced into the eternal night. Rush watched the displays intently as the Titanic approached below them. Everything was still going according to plan. The cameras were transmitting images of the endless blackness, and communication with the surface had been established. During the first hour and a half of the descent, Titan communicated with Polar Prince every 15 minutes. The passengers were eager and excited to see the legendary wreck of the Titanic with their own eyes. They had been preparing for this moment for months and had paid a lot of money for it. The Titan slowly plunged through the cold, dark water, which exerted increasing pressure on her hull. The occupants could see little except the blue glow of the searchlight and the occasional fish or jellyfish swimming past. They talked about their expectations and feelings about the Titanic. But little did they know that they were about to lose their lives. Then suddenly, after a total of 1 hour and 45 minutes in the deep, radio contact was lost. The monitors went black. Full of worry, the crew of the Horizon Arctic tried to reach the Titan - without success. No answer in the eerie silence of the deep sea. The Titan was alone in the darkness, on its way to the Titanic with the Mythos, and communication ceased at 11:15 (13:45 UTC) after a recorded communication.

The bang and the sudden disappearance

Preparations had been in full swing for weeks beforehand. There was supposed to be enough air for 96 hours and the systems for an emergency. And yet disaster struck. The live images went black. Only an unsettling silence returned from the darkness. According to the plan, the submarine should have surfaced at 16:30 (19:00 UTC). But nothing happened.

It was not until 19:10 local time (21:40), more than two hours after the agreed time, that the coastguard was alerted. A feverish search immediately began for the missing ship, whose breathing air reserves were slowly running out. But the Titan remained missing.

James Cameron pointed out that it was likely that the submarine's early warning system had alerted the passengers to an impending delamination of the hull. He added: "We know from inside the community that they had dropped their ascent weights and were coming up to deal with an emergency." A US Navy acoustic detection system designed to locate military submarines detected an acoustic signature consistent with an implosion hours after the Titan submerged.

Had she fallen victim to a sudden calamity? No one wanted to fear it, but the outlook was bleak.

The following catastrophe

Following the disappearance of the Titan on June 18, 2023, the United States Coast Guard, United States Navy and Canadian Coast Guard led the search and rescue efforts. U.S. Air Force and U.S. Guard aircraft, a U.S. Navy ship, and several commercial and research vessels and remotely operated underwater vehicles also assisted in the search. The search included both a surface search and an underwater sonar search. US Coast Guard crews launched search missions 1,700 km from the coast.

All available aircraft and ships were dispatched, some from bases over 1500 kilometers away. In total, the forces combed an area of over 25,000 square kilometers in the first few days. The resources deployed included aircraft such as a Canadian CP-140 Aurora, US C-130 Hercules, a P-8 Poseidon as well as helicopters and ships from the coast guards of both countries.

The weather and the great water depth of over 3000 meters made the search considerably more difficult. While many submersibles are equipped with an acoustic beacon that emits sounds that can be recognized by rescuers underwater, Titan did not have such a device. Nevertheless, the teams continued their efforts tirelessly. Ships with diving robots arrived to search the seabed.

Rear Admiral John Mauger said that they were "using all available means". By the next day, June 19, 2023 10:45 a.m. (13:15 UTC), the US Coast Guard had searched 26,000 km².

According to an internal US government memo, a Canadian aircraft's sonar picked up underwater sounds while searching for the submersible. The US Coast Guard officially confirmed the noises early the following morning, but reported that early investigations had yielded no results. John Mauger of the US Coast Guard said the source of the noise was unknown and could have come from the many metal objects at the site of the wreck. A Canadian plane had earlier spotted a "white rectangular object" floating on the surface. A ship sent to find and identify the object was diverted to find the source of the noise. The noises were later described by the US Coast Guard as apparently unrelated to Titan.

The search continues, and on June 21, additional sonar capabilities were introduced into the search efforts. On this day, the merchant ships also arrived. As of approximately 15:00 (17:30 UTC), five aircraft and vessels were actively searching for Titan. A U.S. Navy ship lift system, designed to lift large and heavy objects from the deep sea, arrived in St. John's, although no ships were available to take the system to the wreck. Officials estimated it would take about 24 hours to weld the so-called underwater crane to the deck of a carrier ship before it could set sail for the search and rescue operation. Despite growing concerns about the depletion of air supplies on Titan if it were intact, a US Coast Guard spokesman told a news conference that "this is 100% a search and rescue mission" and not a wreck salvage mission.

On June 22 at 6:15 p.m. (8:45 p.m. UTC), the U.S. Coast Guard's Northeast Sector announced that another submarine had found a debris field near the wreck of the Titanic. The debris, found five hours into its search, was later confirmed to be part of the submersible. At 16:30 (19:00 UTC) at a US Coast Guard press conference in Boston, the Coast Guard announced that the loss of the submersible was due to an implosion of the pressure chamber and that pieces of titanium were found on the seabed about 500 meters northeast of the Titanic's bow. The debris identified consisted of the stern cone (not part of the pressure vessel) and the forward and aft end bells - both parts of the pressure vessel designed to protect the crew from the marine environment. According to the U.S. Coast Guard, the debris field was concentrated in two areas, with the aft end bell separate from the forward end bell and stern cone.

John Mauger of the U.S. Coast Guard said the debris was consistent with a "catastrophic loss of the pressure chamber." Mauger stated that he did not have an answer as to whether the bodies of those on board would be recovered, but said it was "an incredibly unforgiving environment".

All 5 occupants of the Titan submarine died tragically. The pressure at the depth where the submarine imploded was very high. If you are talking about a depth of over 3000 meters, this is about 400 atmospheres or 6,000 PSI. This is roughly equivalent to the weight of 35 elephants on your shoulders. By comparison, the pressure on the surface is only about one atmosphere or 14.7 PSI. This means that the implosion was so violent that the occupants were probably killed immediately without having time to realize what had happened.

The US Coast Guard and the organizers of the expedition announced to the press in the evening of 23 June that the submarine Titan was lost after a "catastrophic implosion" near the Titanic. All five passengers on board the submersible were killed in the accident. The Titan was on its way to the wreck of the Titanic when it imploded. The wreckage of the submersible has been examined in the USA and medics are now analyzing the presumed human remains that were also recovered. It is unclear how the five passengers died. The interior of the submersible Titan was photographed and published by OceanGate Expeditions. The situation is tragic and dramatic. I extend my deepest condolences to the families and friends of the victims.

6. Fates of no return: The victims of Titan

Stockton Rush

Stockton Rush, the CEO and founder of OceanGate, was born and raised in San Francisco on March 31, 1962. Stockton Rush was born the descendant of two of the founding fathers of the USA. He was fascinated by technology and adventure from an early age. He studied aerospace engineering at Princeton University. Rush obtained his pilot's license at the age of just 19. While still a student, he was allowed to fly huge DC-8 jets over the Atlantic as a co-pilot. After graduating, he worked as a test engineer for US Air Force fighter jets. Along the way, he built his own experimental airplane and a submersible. Rush sat on the board of BlueView Technologies, a sonar manufacturer.

He had been married to Wendy Weil Rush since 1986. She is a great-great-granddaughter of Isidor and Ida Straus, two prominent victims of the sinking of the Titanic.

Rush was sued for fraud in February 2023 by a Florida couple who claimed that their ocean voyage to the Titanic, booked in 2016 and initially scheduled for 2018, had been repeatedly postponed and eventually canceled. Attempts to obtain a refund had been ignored. Rush had defrauded her of 210,000 US dollars. The lawsuit was withdrawn after Rush's death.

Stockton Rush had previously invited his friend Jay Bloom to join his son Sean Bloom on the expedition to the wreck of the Titanic. But when one of young Sean Bloom's friends researched the risks, he warned his friend about it and doubted its safety. Sean asked, "What if a sperm whale attacks the submarine?" Both his father and Rush replied, "Stupid stuff". Still, doubts remained. Rush assured him that the submersible was safe and could even fend off a whale. But the son was not convinced. Jay Blooms would still have to cancel because he had appointments. He said to Rush: "I'll go with you next year. Instead, the places went to entrepreneur Shahzada Dawood and his 19-year-old son Suleman. After the implosion of the Titan submarine, Jay Bloom decided to share chat histories with Stockton Rush with the press. The chat is about his son's safety concerns about the submarine.

Stockton Rush and Wendy Rush had 2 children. Benjamin Rush, who was born in 1988 in San Francisco, currently works as a software engineer for Google and her sister Quincy Rush, who was born in 1991 and studies marine biology.

Stockton Rush died on June 18, 2023 at the age of 61, leaving behind her grieving family.

Hamish Harding

Hamish Harding was born on June 24, 1964 and lived in the United Arab Emirates. He was a resident British entrepreneur and pilot. He was the founder of the Action Group and Chairman of Action Aviation, an international aircraft broker based in Dubai. Harding also visited the South Pole several times, including accompanying astronaut Buzz Aldrin, who in 2016 became the oldest person ever to reach the South Pole at the age of 86. From June 9 to 11, 2019, Harding was mission leader and pilot, together with Terry Virts, of the flight mission comprising around 100 participants to mark the 50th anniversary of the moon landing, setting the world record for the fastest orbit of the Earth over both poles in 46 hours and 40 minutes.

The family of Hamish Harding has spoken out, saying OceanGate waited far too long to raise an alarm and should have reported difficulties at least eight hours earlier, while search and rescue operations continued on Thursday.

After the Titan lost contact with the surface ship, the chairman's cousin, Kathleen Cosnett, expressed her displeasure with the operating company. "It's pretty scary," Kathleen remarked. "They've waited a very long time to come to their rescue. Too much time has passed. I would have expected at least three hours. After I learned that the submarine had lost contact late Sunday." During the night, Hamish's godson Robert Evans said the family had begun calling the British Coastguard and the Foreign Office. This added to Kathleen's worries. Robert, godfather to Hamish's eldest child, continued: "Hamish, his two sons and I are quite close. I think Hamish is a fantastic person. Mind you, I've known him since I was a little kid. He took me skiing, scuba diving and to Machu Picchu, among other exciting places. In short, he was very kind to me. He was a father figure in my life. A surrogate parent, if you will. We are still optimistic. We haven't finished the rescue yet". While Hamish frequently shared his travels on social media, the personal life of Linda, a stay-at-home mom of four, is largely unknown. Before marrying Hamish, Linda had two children, a daughter named Lauren and a boy named Brian, together they have two children named Rory and Giles. The whole family has been seen together a few times, including when Hamish was awarded his second Guinness World Record for circumnavigating the globe in an airplane. Together with his father, Giles maintains an Instagram account called Giles Explores. Hamish Harding was devoted to his family and a loving husband and father to his wife and two sons. When he died, his colleagues at Action Aviation said, "He was one of a kind and we adored him. He was a dedicated family man, company owner and adventurer who sought out new experiences regardless of the terrain.

We know that Hamish would have been immensely proud to see nations, experts, industry colleagues and friends come together for the search. Richard Garriot de Cayeux, a friend of Mr. Harding and current President of the Explorers Club, paid tribute to him. The Explorers Club and I hold Hamish Harding in high regard, as we do Mr. Garriot de Cayeux. He has personally driven kites off the map and supported expeditions and charities, which has earned him several world records. Mr. Harding and Mr. Paul-Henry Nargeolet, he added, were drawn to exploration and did so in the name of meaningful science for the good of humanity.

It wasn't enough for them to simply push themselves in the name of discovery. Mark Hannaford, a Dubai-based member of the Explorers Club, also paid tribute to Mr. Harding, calling him a good father and someone who pushes boundaries.

Hamish Harding died at the age of 58, leaving behind his wife Linda and his two sons Rory and Giles. He was also the stepfather of a daughter Lauren and a son Brian.

Shahzada Dawood and Suleman Dawood

Shahzada Dawood was a Pakistani businessman, investor and philanthropist who was also a citizen of the United Kingdom and Malta. He was Vice Chairman of Engro, a board member of the Dawood Hercules Corporation, a trustee of the Dawood Foundation, the Engro Foundation and the Prince's Trust, and a member of the advisory board of the SETI Institute. An important man for Pakistan. He was married to the German Christine Dawood and had two children with her. Son Suleman Dawood, who also died during the dive on June 18, 2023, and a daughter named Alina.

48-year-old Shahzada Dawood was one of the richest people in Pakistan. Until the end, he lived near London with his wife Christine, who was born in Rosenheim, Bavaria, his son Suleman and his daughter Alina. A photo of the couple together was posted on Facebook the day before. This is no longer available. As Vice Chairman of Engro Corporation, Dawood managed the business of the conglomerate from Karachi in Pakistan. Engro manufactures fertilizers, food, chemicals and petrochemical products. His company Dawood Hercules generated a turnover of 785 million euros in 2020.

Dawood is also said to have been a close friend of the British King Charles III. He was a member of the Global Advisory Board of Prince's Trust International, the King's charity organization. The connection to the royal family had existed for decades, as Dawood's father was one of the founding patrons of the foundation. Partly because of this old connection, the Guardian reports, Buckingham Palace wanted to be kept informed of any new developments in the case of the missing submersible.

Shahzada Dawood was also interested in science. He was a trustee of the Seti Institute in California, which researches the origins of life in space and searches for extraterrestrial life.

The 19-year-old son Suleman is described in the family statement as a "big fan of science fiction literature". He was curious and was enthusiastic about Rubik's cubes and volleyball.
But the son wasn't actually supposed to be there, his mother was. The family has made various statements in interviews about whether the tea manager wanted to go on board the submersible or whether he was afraid of it.

Suleman's mother, Christine Dawood, told the BBC that she was originally supposed to go on the Titan voyage. In the end, she gave her place to her son because he really wanted to go. She went on to say that Suleman wanted to set a world record: solving a Rubik's Cube in the depths of the sea. He is said to have said: "I will solve the Rubik's Cube 3700 meters below sea level on the Titanic and thus set a world record. Christine Dawood says that she was very happy for the two of them, as they had wanted to undertake this journey for a very long time. However, this statement contradicts an interview that Suleman's aunt gave a week before her mother.

Suleman's aunt has spoken out to the US media, saying that her nephew was reluctant to take part in the Titan Expedition. She told NBC News that in the days before the submersible set sail from Newfoundland, he had expressed concerns about whether he should join the expedition at all. He had told a relative that he was "not ready" and was "very scared" of the trip. But the 19-year-old wanted to make his father happy, explained Azmeh Dawood (The Aunt), because the trip was planned for the Father's Day weekend. Shahzada Dawood was passionately interested in the "Titanic" and its history. "It's an unreal situation," Azmeh Dawood continues. "I feel like I'm in a very bad movie.

When I think about them, I can't breathe

>>"*And why does the mother say something different from the aunt? Who should I believe now?*"<<

It's also possible that both are right. It may well be that Suleman wanted to be on board beforehand in order to establish a title and gain recognition. Days before the voyage, his bravery may have waned and he may have considered the safety of the submarine. Nevertheless, he kept his word and went along so as not to disappoint his father.

Christine Dawood wears black. The silence weighs heavily, but she nevertheless talks to the BBC journalist about very emotional topics. The journalist begins with the most difficult question of all: "Christine, can I ask you how you feel? " She answers:
"I've developed a love-hate relationship with the subject. But I have to deal with it. But no, I'm not fine. "

Christine Dawood sometimes looks at the floor, sometimes into space. She searches for words and stutters a little, but she always gives the journalist an answer. She recounts the moment when communication with the Titan submarine was interrupted:

"I don't remember what I was doing, but I was in the belly of the ship when someone came and said, 'We've lost the connection. I never want to hear that phrase again. At first I didn't know what it meant. When I understood it, it got worse and worse. We waited and waited, always hoping that they would return to the surface.

She goes on to say that the members of the expedition team had affirmed that they would climb back up. That it is nothing unusual to lose communication with a vehicle.

Christine Dawood talks about hope, because everyone believed that the Titan would return to the surface. She also explained that there is a time limit for such expeditions. Within 96 hours, i.e. a maximum of four days, until a lost submersible is supposed to surface. Then disaster strikes. They would not return.

" It was only when the 96 hours had passed that I lost hope. "

When Christine talks about her son and her husband, she uses the present tense, as if their deaths were just a figment of her imagination. Christine mentions her daughter, 17-year-old Alina, in a trembling voice: "An incredible young woman. She was also on the ship. She only lost hope when they found the wreckage," says the mother. She says of her late husband: "Shahzada is a history fanatic. He only watches documentaries.

Christine actually wanted to accompany her husband. When the dive was postponed due to the coronavirus pandemic, her son asked to take her place. The journalist asks: "How are you dealing with this? " The widow replies:

"I'd rather not talk about it. "

Shahzada Dawood died at the age of 48 and his son Suleman at the age of 19. A really sad event for the bereaved. We hope that the relatives will find the necessary support and strength.

Let's continue with the last candidate.

Paul-Henry Nargeolet

Paul-Henry Nargeolet was born on March 2, 1946 in Chamonix-Mont-Blanc (France). He was a French deep-sea explorer and Titanic expert. He was known as Mr. Titanic. He spent 13 years of his childhood in Morocco. At the age of nine, he accompanied a group of divers in Casablanca to a cargo ship at a depth of 20 meters. At the age of 16, he returned to France to complete his schooling at the Lycée Jean-Baptiste Say in Paris. From 1964 to 1986, he served in the French Navy, where he was commander of a diving unit for clearing sea mines, a ship's captain and, from 1980, a submarine commander. In the same year, he discovered a Roman wreck off Bonifacio at a depth of 70 meters and explored the 66-gun ship Slava Rossii of the Imperial Russian Navy, which sank off the Île du Levant in 1780.

He was then employed by the French research institute Ifremer as head of the Nautile and Cyana submarine projects until 1996 and carried out the first salvage mission to the Titanic in 1987.

In 1993, he discovered the ship La Lune, which sank in 1664, off Toulon with the Nautile. From 1994, he was director of the newly created Center for Marine & Underwater Resource Management (CMURM) at

Michigan State University. From 1996 to 2003, he also worked for the production company Aqua+, a subsidiary of Canal+, where he managed the underwater missions of two submarines. From 2007, he was Director of the Underwater Research Program at the NASDAQ-listed company.

He led six expeditions to the wreck of the Titanic, during which he supervised the recovery of over 5,000 objects in 30 dives as a submarine guide. In 2010, he took part in the search for the flight recorder of the crashed Air France flight 447 from Rio de Janeiro to Paris.

He was a father to the community when he died. Sidonie Nargeolet, Mr. Titanic's daughter, spoke to reporters and expressed optimism that her father would return from the Titanic voyage. It has not been clarified whether or not he had any other children.

Mr. Titanic died at the age of 77, leaving behind her grieving family. Let's hope the optimistic daughter was able to cope well with the news.

7. Deadly abysses: The search for the truth

Analysis of the possible causes of the accident

The wreckage is evidence that the submarine probably suffered a catastrophic implosion as it descended to the Titanic. The exact cause of the Titan submarine's implosion is not yet known, but there are some possible explanations. The submarine was made of titanium, carbon fiber and fiberglass, all of which should have high strength and corrosion resistance. However, even a small structural flaw or damage in the hull or windows of the submarine could lead to a catastrophic failure.

Submersibles are designed in such a way that they can, or rather must, withstand crushing underwater pressure. Down there, the pressure is around 400 times higher than at sea level.

The implosion would have been very fast and violent, so that the five occupants would have had no chance of surviving or escaping. The implosion would also have caused an enormous build-up of heat, which would have vaporized the submarine and its occupants in a fraction of a second.
If the pressure vessel fails catastrophically, it's like a small bomb exploding. This could destroy all safety devices, explained Stefan Williams, Professor of Marine Robotics.
It was feared that the five passengers on board could be trapped alive in the tiny ship.

However, given the news of the wreckage and a probable implosion, the passengers probably didn't suffer for long: "If this had happened, it would have happened four days ago," said Guillermo Söhnlein, one of the **founders** of **OceanGate**. Do you still remember him? We'll come back to him later.

The implosion would have been almost instantaneous and lasted only milliseconds. Something similar happened in 1961 with the USS

Thresher, a submarine that is believed to have imploded.

The catastrophic event would have pulled the metal ship apart. Complete destruction would occur in a twentieth of a second, too fast for the men in the submarine to cognitively recognize.

An implosion is basically the exact opposite of an explosion. Instead of the pressure moving from the inside out, the pressure flows from the outside in. Similar to an explosion, it is unlikely that much will remain of the ship and its cargo. I know it's not much comfort to the families and spouses, but they were killed instantly. They weren't even aware that anything was wrong.

The implosion of the Titan submarine is a tragic loss for deep-sea exploration and tourism. It raises questions about the safety and reliability of such ventures.

Technical or human error?

Here is an overview of five safety deficiencies of the submarine, which the developers and operators of the submersible are said to have ignored:

1. The fuselage was made of carbon fiber

The "Titan" submarine consisted of two titanium domes joined together by a five-centimeter-thick cylinder made of carbon fiber. According to The Telegraph newspaper, this was an unconventional choice for a deep-sea submersible, which normally has a hull made of stronger materials such as steel or titanium.

The advantage of carbon fibers is that they are much lighter and cheaper. The disadvantage, however, is that they have no compressive strength.

According to a 2018 court filing, OceanGate had been warned of safety risks associated with the use of the material. According to the document, former OceanGate employee David Lochridge expressed concerns about "pressure cycling", where invisible cracks in the hull could lead to larger cracks when exposed to repeated pressure changes.

The CEO of OceanGate, Stockton Rush, even admitted in an interview two years ago that he had "broken some rules" by not using conventional materials. However, Rush didn't want to change anything: "I think I broke them with logic and good engineering. Carbon fiber and titanium? There's a rule that you don't do that," he said in an interview with Mexican YouTuber Alan Estrada in 2021. "Well, I did it," he replied.

2. Concerns regarding the early warning system were ignored

OceanGate advertised the development of an advanced acoustic monitoring system. The technology was intended to provide a timely warning of hull failure. However, in his 2018 analysis, former OceanGate employee Lochridge warned that the detection system was virtually useless - it would only give "milliseconds" of warning of a catastrophic implosion, according to the court filing.

OceanGate refused to follow his recommendation of a "non-destructive examination" of the hull to ensure it was a "sound and safe product for the safety of the passengers and crew," Lochridge's lawsuit states. The company told Lochridge that the Titan's hull was too thick to inspect for weaknesses and adhesion problems.

It is unclear whether Lochridge's concerns were ever addressed or whether OceanGate later conducted the tests he recommended. OceanGate declined to comment on the 2018 letter when asked by The New York Times.

3 OceanGate resisted demands to certify the submarine

What speaks for the lack of safety tests is the testimony of a former passenger: David Pogue, a journalist who boarded the Titan in 2022, said he signed a waiver stating: "This experimental ship was not approved or certified by any regulatory authority." Whether the ship has been certified in the meantime is an open question. But there is no evidence of this.

Instead, former OceanGate employee Lochridge also reports that the ship's forward viewing hatch was only certified to a depth of about 1300 meters, far less than the depth of the Titanic. "The paying passengers were unaware of this experimental design and were not informed of it," Lochridge's lawyers wrote. Outside of OceanGate, the company's handling of the certification also met with criticism: the specialist trade group "Marine Technology Society" wrote to OceanGate in 2018 pointing out that it had listed a certification on its website whose rules it did not comply with.

According to the report, the company's website stated that the ship design would meet or exceed a certification called "DNV-GL".

However, the company does not appear to have made any effort to comply with the certification requirements. The listing on the company's website could be misleading to the public and violates an industry-wide professional code of conduct that we all try to uphold, the Marine Technology Society's letter at the time continued.

In an interview with the New York Times, Will Kohnen, chairman of the Marine Technology Society's Committee on Manned Underwater Vehicles, said: "Their plan to not follow the classification guidelines was considered very risky.
OceanGate CEO Rush later called him to tell him that industry standards were stifling innovation. In a blog from 2019, the company defended its decision not to certify the ship. The reasoning: accidents in shipping and aviation are mostly due to "operator error, not mechanical failure". "Simply focusing on the classification of the ship therefore does not address the operational risks," the company said.

4. OceanGate employees expressed safety concerns but were rebuffed

Former Ocean Gate employee Lochridge was not well after he raised safety concerns about the submersible. The day after he filed his safety report, he was summoned to a meeting with Rush and the company's human resources department, according to the lawsuit. During that meeting, Lochridge was fired and removed from the building.

Lochridge claimed he was fired in retaliation for being a whistleblower.

(A whistleblower is a person who discloses important information from a secret or protected context).

He sued the company in the same year. OceanGate claimed that Lochridge had shared confidential information with external parties. The company described his report as false. Lochridge was not the only one to leave the company over security concerns. Rob McCallum, a researcher and former OceanGate consultant, left the company due in part to concerns that the CEO was over-promising and rushing production. In a recent conversation with Business Insider, McCallum said he was familiar with the equipment used in the Titan submersible and did not think it was safe.

5. There have been previous security incidents

This is not the first time the company has struggled with problems with its submersibles. According to court documents obtained by the New York Times, a 2021 voyage on the Titan was interrupted after battery issues led to the vessel having to be manually attached to its lifting platform.

Pogue, the journalist who traveled on the Titan in 2022, also reported that the ship was lost for several hours while he was on the mother ship. "They were still able to send short texts to the submarine, but they didn't know where it was," Pogue said, "It was quiet and very tense, and they shut down the ship's internet to prevent us from tweeting."

When asked about this by Business Insider, Pogue said that OceanGate had told passengers that the

WiFi had been turned off to free up bandwidth in case the situation developed into an emergency. Pogue also explained that the ship does not have an emergency locator transmitter (ELT) that would send out signals that would allow rescue workers to find the ship. OceanGate did not respond to Business Insider's request for comment by press time.

I think that's proof enough that these are human errors and not technical failures.

Conspiracy theories

This is a sensitive topic that has given rise to much speculation and rumor. According to the search results, there are various conspiracy theories that attempt to explain the implosion of the submarine.

A conspiracy theory claims that the implosion of the submarine Titan was deliberately caused in order to destroy evidence of a secret mission. The mission allegedly consisted of recovering or destroying valuable items from the wreck of the Titanic.

Another conspiracy theory claims that the implosion of the Titan submarine was a planned murder to eliminate one or more of the passengers. The passengers are alleged to have been involved in illegal or dangerous activities, such as espionage, terrorism or organized crime.

Another conspiracy theory claims that the implosion of the Titan submarine was the result of an attack by an unknown enemy who sabotaged or fired on the submarine. The enemy is said to have been a rival of

OceanGate or an opponent of diving trips to the wreck of the Titanic.

However, these conspiracy theories are not supported by facts or evidence and are based on conjecture or prejudice. Most experts and authorities agree that the implosion of the Titan submarine was an accident.

>>"*How do conspiracy theories spread?*"<<

That's a good question. Conspiracy theories are explanations for events or conditions that are based on secret agreements or machinations by powerful groups or individuals. They are often contradictory to scientific findings or official information.

Today, conspiracy theories spread primarily via the internet and are usually passed on by people who use them to "educate" people from their point of view. The aim can be to reach as many people as possible as well as to convince people close to them and their own social contacts.

The internet offers many opportunities to spread conspiracy theories, such as "alternative" news websites, blogs, forums and social networks. These platforms make it possible to share information quickly and easily without checking or questioning it. They can also target specific groups or individuals who are susceptible to conspiracy theories.

Conspiracy theories can also be reinforced by algorithms that suggest content to users that matches their interests or preferences. This can lead to them consuming more and more conspiracy theories and finding themselves in an "echo chamber" or filter bubble in which they only receive information that confirms their opinion.

Conspiracy theories can also be influenced by emotional factors, such as fear, insecurity, anger or frustration. These feelings can lead people to look for simple or plausible explanations for complex or unpleasant situations. Conspiracy theories can give them a sense of control or belonging.

>>"You said that we shouldn't believe everything the media says. But who actually checks that the media is telling us the truth?"<<

There are various ways to check the truth and accuracy of media reports.

Fact check Organizations such as "Correctiv" in Germany or "FactCheck.org" in the USA analyse claims in media reports, for example, and compare them with available data and facts. They specialize in checking the facts. Reputable media outlets also generally cite the sources on which they base their reports. This makes it possible to verify the original sources. If such sources are missing, this can be a warning sign. In a pluralistic media system, different media also monitor each other. If a newspaper spreads false information, it is criticized and corrected by others. This ensures a kind of self-regulation. In Germany, there is also a voluntary self-regulatory body for the press, the German Press Council. Readers can complain there about false reporting. The Press Council then checks whether journalistic due diligence has been observed. Many media also offer the opportunity to give them direct feedback if errors or inaccuracies in reporting are noticed. Attentive readers thus contribute to greater accuracy. Some media also publish annual transparency reports in which they give an account of their work and address errors. There are also scientific studies by universities that analyze and compare the quality of media reporting. They provide information on strengths and weaknesses.

>>*"So the media aren't lying to us after all?"*<<

I didn't say that. I just said how they would do it (according to the law).

The media can certainly disseminate false or misleading information in their reporting. There can be various reasons for this. Sometimes unintentional errors occur because journalists misrepresent facts or place them in the wrong context, especially in daily news reporting. Every journalist also has personal views that can unconsciously influence the selection and weighting of facts. Conflicts of interest can also play a role if the media are dependent on advertising revenue or state funding and can therefore come under pressure to report in the interests of their funders. Governments and other powerful groups can also put pressure on the media to report in their own interests, especially in authoritarian systems. In conflicts, the media may also deliberately spread false information. To increase circulation and ratings, there is also a risk that facts will be distorted or scandals blown out of proportion. It is therefore important to use the media critically and check different sources. However, misinformation in the media can never be completely ruled out.

>>*"And what if the media lie to us and conspiracy theories want to make us aware of the truth?"*<<

Now that piques my curiosity. Tell me, how did you come up with that?

>>"I watched some videos about conspiracy theories on the internet. One of the videos that got me thinking was a video that covered both the Titanic theory and the Titan submarine theory. They showed how many journalists repeat the same phrases in the news. They said it could be that the Titan submarine story was just a red herring to fake her death. That's one of many theories. Overall, it seemed very credible to me. What do you think about it?"<<

I understand what you are trying to tell me. You must understand that the media plays an important role in conveying information. In today's world where information is of great importance, we rely on the media to inform us about current events and historical happenings. This source of information allows us to gain knowledge about past events such as the sinking of the Titanic over 100 years ago.

Although it is important to question the media critically and not blindly believe them, they fulfill a valuable function in society. They give us access to information from all over the world and keep us up to date with what is happening in our society and in the world. Our reliance on the media as a source of information is therefore understandable, as it allows us to be informed citizens and stay up to date.

Let me give you my **personal** take on this ("author's opinion"). I am familiar with many conspiracy theories and tend to believe some of them. This is because I often see the conflicting accounts in the media, and conspiracy theories sometimes seem to be the only explanation. Interestingly, the theories regarding the Titan submarine have not convinced me, and I tend to believe that it was more of an accident in this case. However, I'm not 100% sure about that. I am even more skeptical about the Titanic and suspect that there may be more to the story.

I would like to emphasize that it is important not to blindly believe everything, be it the media or conspiracy theories. Instead, it is advisable to question things critically and examine information carefully.

I advise you to watch the video to hear the other point of view. See what makes more sense to you, but always remain skeptical and don't accept things prematurely. Question them. Who you want to believe is entirely up to you.

I already mentioned that the media often convey important news according to **their opinion** and that's just a point that bothers me.

A boat accident occurred near Greece, in which the authorities believe over 500 people died, a few days before the Titan submarine lost contact with the outside world. The whole world was talking about the submarine and the 500 refugees were neglected.

But what exactly was it about?

The biggest boat accident in migration history

It was a journey into darkness that never ended for many. On June 14, 2023, the fishing vessel Adriana set sail from the Libyan coast to bring hundreds of migrants to Europe. Most of them had fled Africa and the Middle East to escape war, poverty and persecution. They had poured all their money and hopes into the smugglers who promised them a better life.

But the Adriana was not suitable for such a journey. The ship was old, dilapidated and overloaded. The conditions on board were unbearable: There was hardly any water, food or sanitary facilities. The migrants had to squeeze into the cramped spaces without fresh air or protection from the sun. Many suffered from seasickness and infections.

After several days at sea, the ship approached the Greek peninsula of Peloponnese. There it was spotted by a Greek patrol boat, which ordered it to stop and turn back. The Greek authorities did not want to allow any more migrants into the country, as they were already overwhelmed with taking care of thousands of refugees.

They accused Libya of sending the migrants to Europe illegally in order to put pressure on the EU. However, the tugboats on board the Adriana refused to obey the order. They tried to shake off the patrol boat and continue on to Italy. In doing so, they got into a heated argument with the migrants, who were afraid of being taken back to Libya. The situation quickly escalated into panic as some migrants tried to take the wheel or jump into the water.

The ship began to lurch and eventually capsized under the weight of the crowds. The water poured into the ship and dragged many people down with it. Those who made it to the surface screamed for help and clung to debris or life jackets. The patrol boat alerted the coastguard and other rescue services, who launched a large-scale search and rescue operation.

However, the rescue was difficult and dangerous. The sea was stormy and visibility was poor. Many migrants could not swim or were unconscious. Some drowned before they could be reached. Others were attacked by sharks or swept away by the waves. The rescue workers also had to contend with resistance from the traffickers, who tried to destroy evidence or flee.

The rescue operation lasted several days, but hope for survivors dwindled with each passing hour. More than 100 people were rescued alive, but at least 78 people lost their lives. The authorities estimated that over 500 people had died, as many bodies had not yet been recovered. It was one of the biggest or even the biggest boat accident in the history of migration.

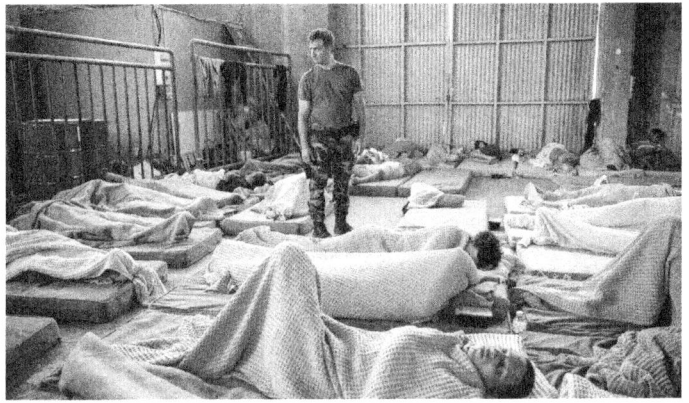

The boat accident triggered a political crisis between Greece and Libya, which blamed each other for the tragedy. The EU called for an investigation into the incident and better coordination of migration policy in the region. The survivors of the accident were housed in various camps where they awaited their asylum procedures or were deported. Many of them suffered from trauma, feelings of guilt and uncertainty about their future.

The boat accident off Greece was a dramatic example of the risks and challenges of migration in the 21st century. It also showed the human cost of a global crisis that requires a common and humane solution. It is likely to be seen as another sad consequence of the ongoing migration crisis that has been going on for many years. Many people had become accustomed to the images of drowning or rescued migrants that regularly appeared in the news. The migrants were often perceived as anonymous masses or numbers with few individual stories or fates. The boat disaster was seen as a political challenge or a humanitarian duty, but not as an emotional issue.

The Titan submarine, on the other hand, was a unique and ambitious project that aimed to push the boundaries of marine research. The submarine was the first to be able to dive to a depth of 4,000 meters and was intended to explore the Titanic and other sunken ships. The mission was accompanied by a great deal of media interest and public fascination, as it was intended to shed new light on the history and mysteries of the deep sea. The submarine accident triggered worldwide sympathy and grief, which pushed the boat accident off Greece into the background. Many people felt a personal connection to the victims of the Titan mission, who were seen as pioneers and heroes. The Titanic was also a symbol of human curiosity and the spirit of adventure that inspired many people. The submarine disaster was perceived as a loss for science and culture.

This is one possible explanation for why the world talked more about the submarine than the boat accident. However, it is important to remember that both accidents cost human lives that had value and dignity.

>>"And why are you (Speacking with Author) writing a book about the Titanic or the Titan submarine and not a book about events such as the Nanggala submarine, the Wilhelm Gustloff, or, as you are telling us, the sad story of the refugees on the boat off Greece? You said that the media themselves decide what news they consider important, and yet you focus on the famous events. Yet you yourself neglect the other events. That's contradictory."<<

Nevertheless, I decided to focus my book on the Titanic and the Titan submarine because this topic appeals to readers more and therefore reaches a wider readership. This is because the Titanic is widely known and fascinating, which makes people naturally curious.

However, that doesn't mean that I ignore the other events. I also mentioned the stories of the Wilhelm Gustloff, the submarine Nanggala and the refugee disaster off Greece to inform readers about the reality.

My aim is to make those who read the book because of Titanic or Submarine Titanic aware of these often overlooked tragedies. I want readers to think about the reality and the lesser known events. It's sad, but the fact is that few people care about these neglected events, and most tend to prefer books about more popular topics.

By including these stories in my book, I want to emphasize that we must not forget these neglected events, even if they may initially arouse less interest. It is a way to spread the message that these stories deserve attention. These stories are just as tragic as the Titanic or the implosion of the Titan submarine.

8. Into the unknown: Marine technology expedition

Progress with submersibles and robots

We have long dreamed of exploring the mysterious depths of the oceans. But the gigantic pressure and darkness of the deep sea seemed to present almost insurmountable barriers. Only with the greatest engineering skill was it possible to gradually develop submersible underwater boats that could withstand these extreme conditions.

The early models from the 1930s onwards hardly resembled the agile deep-sea robots of today. They were clunky steel cylinders with small portholes. But they were a start. With each expedition, the designers gathered new insights to increase safety, maneuverability and diving depth.

One particular challenge was the submersibles' resistance to pressure as the depth of the sea increased. At a depth of just a few hundred meters, the pressure is many times higher than the air pressure on the surface. Without an extremely resistant hull, a U- boat hull would be crushed like an aluminum can. The air-independent energy supply also had to be rethought.

It was the advances in light metals, accumulators and later even nuclear drives that opened up new possibilities. Step by step, engineers expanded our radius of action. Thanks to pioneering designs, modern submersibles can now even reach the Mariana Trench, the deepest point of the oceans.

Robotic arms, grippers and high-tech instruments have also greatly expanded the research possibilities. Even gigantic deep-sea creatures can be studied at close range. And thanks to video cameras and live transmissions, we can even climb on board virtually.

The vastness of the oceans remains a challenge. But the inquisitive creativity of engineers is gradually giving us a glimpse into these unique habitats. With each expedition, we are able to open up the treasures of the deep sea a little more. Even if much still remains unexplored, we venture into an exciting underwater world with a pioneering spirit.

>>"What is the current state of exploration of our oceans?"<<

The oceans cover over 70% of the Earth's surface and are home to a breathtaking diversity of life. But a large part of the underwater world is still hidden. Only a fraction has been explored so far.

We already have relatively comprehensive knowledge of the near-shore zones and areas close to the surface. Marine life and habitats can be studied here by snorkeling and diving. However, these regions make up less than 10% of the total surface area.

The twilight zone begins for us at depths of 200 meters or more, where only special diving boats can penetrate. Fantastic creatures such as giant octopuses and luminous jellyfish can be found here. But the difficulties of exploration increase with every depth.

Over 50% of the seabed is located at depths of over 3000 meters. Extreme pressures of over 300 kilograms per square centimeter prevail here. Without high-tech submarines, this area is inaccessible. Our knowledge of the deep sea world is correspondingly limited.

Even modern systems such as remote-controlled diving robots or underwater drones have only been able to explore a fraction of these vast expanses. New species are discovered on every deep-sea expedition. It is estimated that over 90% of the oceans are still unexplored.

So we have only just begun to uncover the secrets of the oceans. Countless breathtaking discoveries still await us. Thanks to new technologies, we can now decode this unknown habitat step by step. The fascination remains boundless. We are ready for the next dive into an exciting underwater world full of wonders.

Drones, 3D mapping and virtual tours

Marine research has benefited from the use of drones and 3D mapping in recent years. Drones can be used to monitor the ocean surface and collect data useful for marine research. 3D mapping can be used to map the topography of the seabed and understand the structure of the seabed. Virtual tours can be used to give users a better understanding of the marine environment.

The use of drones in marine research has many advantages. They can be used to monitor the ocean surface and collect data that is useful for marine research. For example, they can be used to measure the temperature of the water, salinity and other important parameters. They can also be used to observe animals in the sea and track their movements.

3D mapping can be used to map the topography of the seabed and understand the structure of the seabed. This is particularly useful for exploring underwater mountains and valleys and for identifying reefs and other underwater structures. 3D mapping can also help to better understand the influence of tides and currents on the sea.

Virtual tours can be used to give users a better understanding of the marine environment. They can be used to conduct virtual dives or to provide users with an interactive tour of different parts of the ocean.

There is a new AI fish robot called Belle that has been developed by ETH Zurich to study fish in their natural environment. The robot is equipped with a camera with which it can take pictures of fish.

These images are then analyzed to gather information about the fish's behaviour. The robot is designed to move like a fish, enabling it to approach the fish without disturbing them. The robot can also be used to record data about the environment, helping to improve understanding of the marine environment.

Artificial intelligence and big data from the ocean

In recent years, marine research has benefited from the use of artificial intelligence (AI) and big data. Big data refers to the large amount of information that can no longer be handled by conventional analysis methods. Modern big data analytics approaches describe how complex high-level phenomena emerge from interactions at smaller levels and what patterns emerge. In this way, research investigates how interactions and changes at the genetic, neuronal, systems and behavioral levels, as well as socio-demographic and environmental factors, affect the cognitive processes that are disturbed in patients. Computer-aided models and machine learning methods are required to analyze such large, high-dimensional and complex data sets. The term "big data" therefore covers not only the data itself, but also the tools for data collection, indexing and retrieval (databases, pattern recognition, statistics, etc.).AI can be used in marine research to collect and analyze data.

Overall, AI and big data have the potential to improve our understanding of the ocean and help us better understand the challenges of climate change.

9. Ambition and hope: lessons for eternity

The future of OceanGate

However, there are some possible scenarios that could occur in relation to OceanGate and the Titan submarine:

1. **OceanGate**: OceanGate could continue to conduct deep-sea expeditions and make new discoveries. They could improve their technology and equipment to enable even deeper dives. They may discover new species of marine life or explore previously unexplored areas of the ocean.

2. **Titan submarine**: Following the tragic accident involving the Titan submarine, a thorough investigation could be carried out to determine the exact cause of the implosion. The results of this investigation could lead to future deep-sea submersibles being built more safely. It is also possible that other companies or organizations could make models of the submarine and exhibit them in museums. The recovered debris could also end up in the museum.

3. **Titanic expedition**: The expeditions to the wreck of the Titanic could be continued, either with modified versions of the submarine or with other submersibles. These expeditions could help to learn more about the wreck and gain new insights into the history of the Titanic

It will be interesting to see what happens in the future, as there are many unknown factors that could influence developments.

The fate of OceanGate after the accident

Following the accident involving the Titan submarine, OceanGate has completely suspended all exploration and commercial activities. The US Coast Guard is leading an investigation into the accident with the participation of Canada, France and the United Kingdom.

Guillermo Söhnlein, the other founder of OceanGate, has spoken publicly after the accident. In an interview with the New York Times, he said that he was "devastated" and that the company would "do everything we can to make sure this never happens again". He also emphasized that the company had "always maintained the highest safety standards" and that the accident was "a tragedy for everyone involved". But OceanGate is not his only project.

It is unclear whether OceanGate will ever carry out deep-sea expeditions again. The company announced on its website that it had ceased "all exploration and commercial activities". Shortly afterwards, the website was no longer accessible. OceanGate did not initially provide any further details. However, it is possible that the company will continue to carry out deep-sea expeditions and make new discoveries in the future. Guillermo wants to continue working to explore the wreck of the Titanic. They may improve their technology and equipment to enable even deeper dives. It is also possible that other companies or organizations will develop and deploy similar submersibles.

It remains to be seen how the future of OceanGate will develop. However, it is certain that the accident with the Titan submarine has left a deep wound in the deep-sea exploration community.

Guillermo Söhnlein's Venus Project 2050

As crazy as it sounds, Söhnlein, the co-founder of OceanGate, has an amazing and crazy plan. Despite misfortune during a dive, Söhnlein wants to go even higher. Now the entrepreneur is apparently reaching for the stars and wants to send people to Venus.

Guillermo Söhnlein is an Argentinian-American entrepreneur who is best known as the co-founder of the deep-sea exploration company OceanGate.

He was born on May 18, 1966 in Buenos Aires, Argentina. In 1972, he emigrated with his family to the United States, where they settled in San Jose, California. He attended St. Francis High-School in Mountain View and became a naturalized citizen in 1986. He studied at the University of California at Berkeley, where he earned a bachelor's degree in economics in December 1989. In May 1995, he earned a Juris Doctor from the University of California Hastings College of the Law in San Francisco, where he was editor-in-chief of the West-Northwest Journal of Environmental Law and Policy.

From 1995 to 1999, he served in the United States Marine Corps and reached the rank of Captain. In 1998, he founded Milo, a speech recognition technology company that was acquired by Voxeo in 2001. After relocating to the Northern Virginia region outside of Washington, D.C., he worked with several technology start-up companies and advised several technology-related investment groups, incubators and economic development agencies. He also lectured frequently about the field.

In 2003, he founded the International Association of Space Entrepreneurs (IASE), a non-profit organization designed to encourage successful entrepreneurs from other industries to found aerospace-related companies and start-ups. The group grew from five people to almost 1,500 people around the world. In 2010, the online community was transferred to the Space Frontier Foundation for further growth, and the IASE officially disbanded. In 2006, he founded the Space Angels Network, a for-profit angel investor group for early-stage aerospace companies.

In 2009, he founded OceanGate together with Stockton Rush. He left the company in 2013, but retained a minority stake. He was one of the first pilots of the submersible Cyclops 1, which could dive to a depth of 500 meters. He was also involved in the development of the Titan submersible, but exploring the oceans is not his only goal. He has not been discouraged by recent events and maintains that humanity must continue to push the boundaries of innovation.

Söhnlein is planning a trip around the brightest planet we can see in the evening sky. Around 1,000 people are to travel into the atmosphere to the second closest planet to the sun by 2050. Modesty in this plan is obviously alien to him. "I think it's less ambitious than sending a million people to the surface of Mars by 2050," he told Business Insider, alluding to Elon Musk's plans. He expects his idea to cause a stir both inside and outside the space industry.

The project is probably also spectacular because Venus is close to Earth in terms of size, but not in terms of quality of life. The lump of rock has a surface temperature of 400 degrees and an atmospheric pressure that liquefies the air. It could only be bearable for humans at altitudes of around 50 kilometers.

This is exactly where Söhnlein wants to send his spaceships and build a station. Another problem: it has to withstand the sulphuric acid in the atmosphere of Venus. But these are probably details that the businessman has not yet dealt with. "I think I've been driven to make humanity a planet-spanning species since I was eleven," he says, "I've always had the dream of being the commander of the first Mars colony".

OceanGate had tried to develop cheap submersibles that could be used to reach the seabed. Söhnlein could also want to use the technological approach developed in the process for journeys into space. Together with entrepreneur Khalid Al-Ali, Söhnlein has launched the "Humans2Venus" project to overcome commercial obstacles to a flight to Venus, according to the "Business Insider" report. He is apparently taking inspiration from Elon Musk, whose company SpaceX has significantly reduced the cost of rockets.

Cost reduction was probably also an important factor for OceanGate. When developing the submersibles, the usual use of titanium steel was dispensed with and carbon fiber was used. Among other things, experts accused OceanGate of failing to have the boat certified. According to the report, Söhnlein saw certification as an illusion of safety. He was convinced that researchers had to take calculated risks in their ventures.

Söhnlein sees the most important argument for the selection of Venus in the planet's gravity. "I am not an engineer or a scientist, but I believe in the ability of both professions," he writes on his website. They could overcome many challenges. But there is one exception: gravity. And at an altitude of 50 kilometers in the atmosphere of Venus, it is the same as on Earth.

A few years ago, NASA had already investigated whether it would be possible to live in the atmosphere of Venus. However, the "Havoc" project was more of a concept study on how to explore the solar system. "If you look at what technologies need to be developed for HAVOC, it can be applied to other missions to the Moon, Mars and beyond. All of this work is interrelated and our ability to realize projects in space is improving," said project leader Christ Jones, describing the intentions.

Söhnlein is therefore a versatile and visionary entrepreneur who is passionate about both the deep sea and outer space. He has founded or co-founded several companies involved in various aspects of exploration. He also has an academic background in business and law and a military background in the Marine Corps.

But how do you see the whole thing?

>>"Do you mean me?" <<

Yes, who am I telling this to?

>>"Oh yeah, really crazy. The guy was involved in the implosion of the Titan submarine, where people died, and he doesn't seem to care. He uses people like they're guinea pigs. He has a lot of research goals, but you can see what came out of the Titanic expedition. Before he invites others to join him, perhaps he should fly to Venus himself and return safely. If he succeeds, he can involve others in his projects." <<

Exploring the oceans of the future

The oceans are the largest and most mysterious habitats on our planet. They cover more than 70% of the Earth's surface and are home to millions of species, many of which are still undiscovered. The oceans play an important role in climate, food security, the economy and human health. Yet despite their importance, the oceans are still poorly studied and understood.

Further research into the oceans is therefore of great importance in order to overcome the many challenges we face in the 21st century. By exploring the oceans, we can learn more about the biodiversity, ecosystems, resources and threats of the oceans. We can also develop new technologies, medicines, materials and energy sources from the sea. In addition, we can better understand how climate change affects the oceans and how we can combat it.

However, researching the oceans requires close cooperation between different disciplines, institutions, countries and sectors. It also requires a high level of investment in scientific infrastructure, equipment, personnel and data management. And it needs strong public awareness and participation to raise awareness of the importance and beauty of the oceans.

The oceans are a source of life, knowledge and inspiration for us all. They are also a shared heritage and a shared responsibility. By continuing to explore the oceans, we can not only learn more about them, but also more about ourselves.

Some examples of future projects and initiatives in ocean research are:

- **The Ocean Decade**: The United Nations has declared 2021-2030 the Decade of Ocean Science for Sustainable Development. The aim is to strengthen international cooperation to promote ocean science, increase capacity, inform policy and raise public awareness. The Ocean Decade has ten societal goals that relate to issues such as conserving biodiversity, reducing pollution, adapting to climate change and improving human health.

- **The Seabed 2030 Initiative**: This initiative was launched in 2017 to achieve complete mapping of the seabed by 2030. Currently, only about 20% of the seabed is mapped, which means we know more about the surface of the moon than the bottom of our own oceans. The Seabed 2030 initiative aims to close this gap by collecting and integrating data from different sources to create a high-resolution global map of the seafloor. This map will help us learn more about the geology, biology, history and dynamics of the oceans.

- **The Starfish 2030 mission**: This mission was proposed by the European Commission in 2020 to achieve a healthy and resilient ocean by 2030. The Starfish 2030 mission has five objectives: clean the ocean, protect the ocean, regenerate the ocean, harvest the ocean and understand the ocean. To achieve these goals, the mission aims to take a number of actions, such as creating marine protected areas, restoring ecosystems, promoting sustainable fisheries and aquaculture, developing a circular economy and involving citizens in ocean research and education.

These and other initiatives show the potential and need for further research into the oceans in the future. Ocean research is not only a scientific task, but also a social obligation. By continuing to explore the oceans, we can not only learn more about them, but also more about ourselves.

The possible disappearance of the Titanic

The Titanic, which was considered an unsinkable ship, sank in the North Atlantic over 100 years ago. The wreck of the Titanic has been lying on the seabed at a depth of over 3,800 meters ever since. But experts are now sounding the alarm: the Titanic could soon disappear forever!

Scientists for polar and marine research estimate that the remains of the ship could have completely disintegrated in 15 to 20 years. The cause of this is bacterial iron corrosion, which decomposes the ship's metal. The bacteria, named Halomonas titanic after the place where they were found, extract electrons from the iron as a source of energy in order to grow. This causes the metal to rust and become porous. The bacteria also cause holes, which makes the wreck unstable and leads to its collapse.

The wreck of the Titanic is covered in biofilm and rust, which is changing its original shape. Some parts of the ship have already disappeared or are damaged, such as the mast or the bridge. The environmental conditions in the deep sea, such as high pressure, low temperature, salt water and currents, are also contributing to the deterioration of the wreck. The Titanic is therefore slowly but surely being reclaimed by nature.

Researchers are trying to counteract this fate. The wreck is constantly being examined and documented with the help of diving robots and scanners. But the possibilities are limited. The salt water in the depths is aggressive. All that can be observed is how the famous wreck slowly disintegrates in the darkness.

The Titanic is not only a historical testimony, but also a symbol of the limits of human technology and respect for nature. Its disappearance would be a great loss for mankind, but also a reminder that nothing is made to last forever.

>>"But isn't it better if the Titanic disappears? Then something like the implosion of the Titan submarine, where people lost their lives, can be avoided. And a lot of money will be saved, which could be invested in vital resources." <<

That's a good point. The disappearance of the Titanic could also have positive aspects:

- There would be no more dangerous expeditions to the wreck. There have been fatal accidents in the past when exploring the Titanic, as was the case with the Titan submarine. If the wreck can no longer be reached, such risks will be avoided.
- The high costs of researching and documenting the Titanic could be saved. Experts estimate that over 100 million dollars have been spent on investigating the wreck so far. This money could be put to better use for humanitarian purposes.

- There are fears that the Titanic could be salvaged and exhibited for financial gain. The disappearance would forestall this.

Whether the benefits of disappearing outweigh the cultural losses is certainly debatable. In any case, you have raised an important aspect that should be considered. There are certainly arguments that natural disappearance could also be positive.

Others claim that the disappearance of the Titanic is a cultural and scientific loss that should be prevented. The Titanic is a testimony to the history, technology and society of the early 20th century. It contains much information that has not yet been researched or documented. If the Titanic disappears, this information will be irretrievably lost. Furthermore, it could be said that the disappearance of the Titanic diminishes the significance of the shipwreck and the victims. The Titanic would become a myth that exists only in speculation and fantasy.

>>*"Couldn't the Titanic be pulled out with today's technology? And if so, why not do it?"*<<

The question of whether the Titanic could be salvaged with today's technology is not easy to answer. There are various factors that make salvage difficult or even impossible. Here are some of them:

The depth: The Titanic lies at a depth of over 3800 meters at the bottom of the Atlantic Ocean. This means that the water pressure there is around 400 bar. That is about 400 times higher than on the surface. To get to the wreck, you need special submersibles or robots that can withstand the high pressure. These are very expensive and rare.

The destruction: The Titanic broke in two during the sinking and was further damaged when it hit the seabed. In addition, the metal of the ship is decomposed by bacteria, which make it rusty and porous. The wreck is therefore very unstable and would probably fall apart or crumble if salvaged.

The size: The Titanic was one of the largest ships of its time. It was around 270 meters long and 28 meters wide. To salvage her, huge cranes or lifting equipment would be needed to carry the enormous weight of the wreck. These would also have to be adapted to the depth and the currents. Such equipment does not yet exist, or only in very limited numbers.

The costs: Salvaging the Titanic would be a very complex and costly undertaking. The search for the wreck alone cost several million dollars. A salvage operation would require much more money that could be used for other purposes. It would also be necessary to clarify who owns the wreck and who is responsible for salvaging it. This could lead to legal disputes.

The ethics: The Titanic is not only a historic wreck, but also a mass grave. Around 1500 people lost their lives in the disaster. Many of them still lie in or around the wreck. A salvage operation would disturb this resting place and possibly damage or lose the remains of the victims. That would be disrespectful and inappropriate.

For these reasons, the Titanic will probably not be salvaged. She will continue to lie at the bottom of the sea and be slowly reclaimed by nature. That may be a shame, but perhaps it is for the best. The Titanic is a symbol of the limits of human technology and respect for nature. Her disappearance would be a great loss to humanity, but also a reminder that nothing is made to last forever.

Summary of the findings

Having dealt so extensively with the Titanic, its sinking and the subsequent discovery of the wreck, we have to ask ourselves: what is the main message of this whole story?

One thing is clear: the Titanic was the pride of the engineers at the time, a marvel of technology. People thought that nothing could harm this giant ship. But the subsequent sinking showed the world in a brutal way: In the end, nature is mightier than any ocean liner, no matter how big.

The diving boats that discovered the wreck decades later were also attracted by this myth. Exploring the deep sea remains a risky undertaking to this day. This was tragically demonstrated by the sinking of the submersible Titan, which set off for the Titanic in 2023 and imploded.

The story of the Titanic and its technical successor Titan teaches us not to underestimate the forces of nature and to accept our limits. But also never to lose our pioneering spirit and to keep looking ahead.

If we learn from this, the memory of the Titanic and its passengers will stay alive forever. Right?

>>"*In any case*"<<

Epilogue

Our journey ends where it began - in the depths of the ocean. A journey that took us into the past and the future at the same time. We followed visionary pioneers and witnessed tragedies. But what remains when the last page is turned?

This story has shown us that boundaries should sometimes be crossed in order to discover new things. But also that the forces of nature will always win out in the end if we are not aware of the risks. As much as we humans strive for knowledge, we must never forget humility.

This story also raises fundamental questions beyond the specific case. Why does the fate of some victims receive so much more public sympathy than that of others? Are we biased in our compassion? Everyone deserves the same empathy, regardless of their background or status.

Perhaps this imbalance reminds us to take a closer look and care more comprehensively. In a just world, the suffering of everyone would be seen and mourned equally, instead of just less. That is the challenge for all of us - not to forget where our attention is lacking.

One thing is certain: curiosity remains. So many secrets still lie dormant in the depths of the oceans. There are still horizons to be explored that seem unimaginable today. This longing for the unknown has always driven mankind. Our journey has come to an end and is beginning anew at the same time.

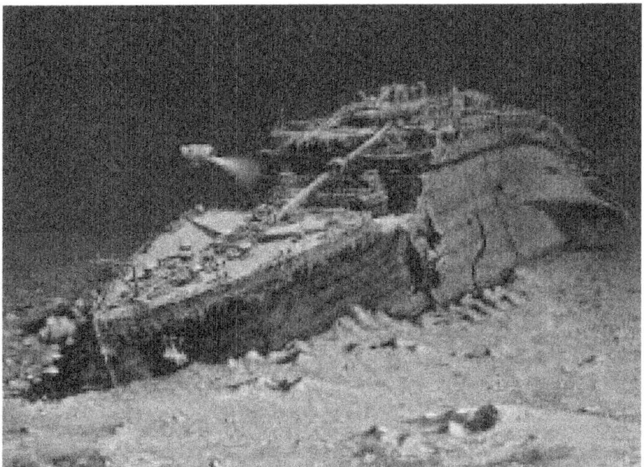

Many thanks for your support

I would like to thank you all from the bottom of my heart for your wonderful support. It fills me with joy and gratitude to see how my book has been received by you.

Your positive feedback and reviews have been incredibly enriching to my work as an author. It has been a fascinating journey to share my work with you and your interest in it means a lot to me.

This book would not be the same without you. Thank you for reading my stories, sharing your thoughts and letting my words into your lives.

I look forward to staying in touch with you and hope that my future works will inspire you just as much.

Yusuf Fadel

Fadel

Printed in Great Britain
by Amazon